FOURTH OF JULY FORGERY

A HOLIDAY COZY MYSTERY

BOOK SIX

TONYA KAPPES

TONYA KAPPES
WEEKLY NEWSLETTER

Want a behind-the-scenes journey of me as a writer?
The ups and downs, new deals, book sales, giveaways and more? I share it all! Join the exclusive Southern Sleuths private group today! Go to www.patreon.com/Tonyakappesbooks

As a special thank you for joining, you'll get an exclusive copy of my cross-over short story, *A CHARMING BLEND.* Go to Tonyakappes.com and click on subscribe at the top of the home page.

PREVIEW

As the grand finale erupted in a shower of shimmering sparks, we sat in silence, our hearts filled with gratitude and wonder. The sounds of the cheers and applause from the crowd below reached our ears, a testament to the joy and delight the fireworks had brought to everyone in Holiday Junction.

Then some screaming suddenly took over the cheers. Darren and I stood up to see why.

"What's going on?" I asked, leaning over the railing.

As a journalist with an insatiable curiosity, I couldn't help but dart off back down the stairs to get an up-close and personal photo of whatever was going on.

I took a deep breath, allowing the salty breeze to fill my lungs, heightening my senses. The stage was set, the atmosphere charged with anticipation.

Little did I know that by the end of this night, the vibrant celebration would give way to a grim discovery, plunging Holiday Junction into a web of secrets and intrigue.

As soon as we reached the beach, one last burst of fireworks illuminated the darkening sky, and I felt a surge of adrenaline, knowing that my nose for news and the light of the fireworks would lead me straight into the heart of the unfolding mystery.

At the time, I didn't realize it was a dead body on the beach.

CHAPTER ONE

Under the twilight sky, as the colorful sparks of fireworks danced above, the quaint town of Holiday Junction came alive with a symphony of laughter, joy, and the captivating warmth of an ocean breeze to celebrate the first day of the Fourth of July Festival.

I was perched at my desk in the *Junction Journal* office, overlooking the bustling scene unfolding outside. The ocean's salty aroma wafted through the open windows, mingling with the excitement and anticipation that hung in the air.

"Violet, are you 'bout done?" my mama, Millie Kaye, asked. She was southern to her core and brimmed with enthusiasm for any celebration that came our way.

She popped her head into the door of my office.

I had to keep myself from laughing as I took in an outfit I'd call gaudy, but she'd call it getting into the spirit of the Fourth of July.

Mama had carefully selected an ensemble that exuded patriotic flair. She wore a flowy navy-blue maxi dress adorned with white stars, its fabric swaying gently as she headed straight over to my desk with something in her fingers.

The dress was cinched at the waist with a vibrant red belt, which added a touch of boldness to her ensemble. She had a straw hat tucked underneath her arm.

"I've got my brochures just in time." She wagged the object in the air and handed it to me, giving me an even better look at it—a pair of dazzling earrings crafted in the shape of sparkling fireworks. Her pocketbook was in the crook of her elbow.

The earrings dangled delicately, each burst capturing the essence of the celebratory fireworks that would soon light up the night sky.

"Look at what a bang-up job Clara and Garrett did down at the Printing Press." She pointed at the front of the brochure, showing that even her nails had fireworks painted on them. "We bartered."

She was lit up like a sparkler at the memory of making this deal.

"And what did you agree upon, Mama?" I asked.

"They gave me a steep discount on the printing in full color, and I gave them three months of free membership at the Leisure Center." Mama popped the straw hat on top of her head.

The hat was adorned with a wide red ribbon. A small American flag pin was pinned on the ribbon, a subtle yet powerful symbol of her patriotism.

She snapped the top of her purse open, took out a handful of the brochures, and slapped them down on my desk.

"Now, me and you are going to be giving these out tonight," she told me with a warm smile and a twinkle in her eye.

"Okay, Mama." I got up and noticed her comfortable-looking yet stylish white sandals adorned with red and blue accents.

It was Mama's way of having the perfect balance between fashion and practicality, ensuring she could navigate the festivities with ease. Mama never did anything without thinking through the outfit she would wear for any event.

"You aren't going out there lookin' like that, are you?" she asked. Then she must have realized what she'd said, because she gasped slightly and knotted her brows. "You look all right. Besides, it's getting dark out soon. And, well"—her lips pinched—"everyone will be looking at the fireworks instead of you."

That was Mama's way of apologizing. Her southern way. I'd gotten used to it over the years. She loved me, and I knew it, or she'd never have followed me to Holiday Junction when I moved here a little over a year ago. Just about a month later, she showed up at my door with her suitcase in hand, just landed from our home in Normal, Kentucky.

I figured she was going to stay for one week, maybe two. Boy, was I wrong. She not only stayed but ended up buying a house. Then my daddy moved here. Soon, she started working with me at the *Junction Journal.*

Now she was opening up the Leisure Center because she said Holiday Junction needed a place for seniors to go, though she refused to call it that.

"I'm not going to say anything, but I love the you-know-what." Her words ran together.

"Mama," I said in a tone that told her not to say another word.

"I know, I know." She sighed. "I'm going to use the ladies' room, so get your stuff and let's go."

"Yeah, yeah." When I walked over to get my camera bag, I stopped at the window and looked out at the beach.

As I gazed out of the office window, my heart fluttered with excitement and anticipation. The Fourth of July festivities were in full swing, and as the co-Merry Maker of Holiday Junction with Darren Strickland, it was my responsibility to ensure the holiday celebration's grand finale was nothing short of spectacular.

The Merry Maker was one of the most important jobs, if not *the* most important, in Holiday Junction, and it was secret. No one, well, no one but Darren, Mama, Vern McKenna, and I knew we were the current Merry Makers.

Darren, with his warm smile and unwavering enthusiasm, was not only my partner in merrymaking but also someone with whom I had developed a budding relationship.

We shared a deep connection and a love for this charming town. It was no surprise that he called the lighthouse his home, a symbol of guidance and strength that overlooked the picturesque coastline.

Together, Darren and I had meticulously planned the holiday's last hurrah, a gathering that would bring the townsfolk together for one final moment of joy and camaraderie.

Our chosen location for this year's festivities was the beach, and to mark the spot, we had placed a magnificent ten-foot sparkly rocket that shone and shimmered in the fading daylight. Vern had made the rocket for us using his amazing skills as a carpenter.

This iconic symbol of the large rocket held a special meaning for the townspeople, signifying that the heart of the celebration would unfold right here, where the crashing waves met the sandy shore. In this place, laughter would echo, memories would be made, and the spirit of community would be ignited.

As the sun began its descent, casting a warm golden glow across the beach, I couldn't help but feel a swell of pride. The atmosphere crackled with anticipation, and the townsfolk knew, without a doubt, that this was the place to be, the epicenter of the evening's revelry.

Children ran along the shoreline, their laughter mixing with the sound of crashing waves. Families set up picnic blankets, their mouths watering in anticipation of the delicious food and sweet treats that would be shared. The air was filled with the cheerful chatter of friends and neighbors, the people's faces painted with expressions of joy and excitement.

"You ready?" Mama asked, bringing me out of the nostalgia I'd entered. "Violet?"

"Yep." I grabbed the camera bag from the shelf and turned around. "I'm going to get some great photos for tomorrow's special Fourth of July edition of the *Junction Journal*."

Mama led me all the way down the sidewalk in front of all the seaside shops, giving her brochures to anyone who extended a hand.

"Darlin', can you believe the turnout we're havin' for the Fourth of July festivities?" Mama exclaimed, her eyes sparkling with joy.

She'd stopped at Popcorn Paradise. The food stand offered a variety of popcorn flavors, from traditional buttery popcorn to gourmet options like caramel, cheese, and even spicy flavors.

"The fireworks display is gonna be a real showstopper this year, and I'm hopin' folks will come check out the Leisure Center while they're at it." Mama turned and looked back over her shoulder to see what I was staring at. "Do you want some popcorn?"

"I think I will, so you go on and I'll meet you at the Merry Maker sign," I suggested because she clearly wanted to hand out all those brochures.

"Don't forget to hand those out. I don't want to see a single one in your hand when I meet you." She made sure I understood what she expected of me before she took off down the sidewalk.

As I stood in line, I couldn't help but take out my camera to snap a few candid shots of children eating some of the festival foods. The kids were sitting on the curb of the street that had been blocked off by the Holiday Junction Police Department.

My mouth watered when I realized I was next in line, and my eyes focused on the caramel popcorn option.

"One small caramel popcorn, please," I told the young man who asked to take my order. He stood behind a small screen window barely cracked open.

"Make it a large," a familiar voice boomed behind me. The speaker's hand placed a ten-dollar bill in the sliding window.

With a contented sigh, I turned to Darren. Our eyes met for a brief moment, sharing unspoken understanding and excitement.

"I've been looking for you." His dark eyes framed by his thick brows sent my heart into a crazy butterfly spiral. He raised his other hand, which held the Leisure Center brochure. "I saw Millie Kay. She said you were at Popcorn Paradise."

"I'm so glad you found me." I tried to keep my smile small, but it was as large as the fireworks display would be. He looked so cute in his brown longboard-style shorts, loose long-sleeved white shirt with the sleeves rolled up, and dock shoes.

He was so laid-back with his dressing style and long hair that he was good for me.

I took the popcorn from the guy behind the window. Darren and I stepped away from the stand.

"Look around at all the happy faces." He took a handful of caramel popcorn, popping a few kernels in his mouth.

"We did good this time." I shoved a handful of the delicious treat in my mouth, agreeing we'd finally found a good rhythm for where the secret Merry Maker spot for each holiday would be hosted. Previously, we'd never agreed on where they should be.

With mouths full of popcorn, Darren and I took the moment to glance at our surroundings. This was our way to bring happiness and unity to the people we cherished.

Together, we'd create a night to remember, a night when the spirit of the Fourth of July would shine as brightly as the stars above us.

"Let's go get a front-row beach seat," Darren said. He started to lead me down the road to the big wooden rocket, walking with the rest of the crowd.

We took our time so I could stop and snap photos of all the food vendors.

The Beachside Grill was a cute stand that served juicy burgers, hot dogs, and smoky barbecued chicken. Everything there looked like it was expertly cooked to perfection.

Seafood Shack was another cute stand serving fresh catches from the ocean and a variety of other seafood delights, from succulent shrimp skewers and crispy fish tacos to creamy clam chowder and mouthwatering lobster rolls. The owners boasted that seafood lovers were in for a delectable treat.

"You can wash that down with one of those." I pointed at the Lemonade Oasis stand and watched Darren scarf down a shrimp skewer.

Of course, there was a booth for people who wanted more sweets than the caramel popcorn stand offered.

Sweet Treats Delight had a display of cotton candy, caramel apples, chocolate-dipped strawberries, and colorful candy floss. You could imagine how long the line was when we walked past.

"I think I got some really good candids for the morning paper." I quickly flipped through the digital photos to show Darren before we took off our shoes and walked on the sandy beach.

"It's really crowded." Darren had stopped. He towered over almost everyone's heads as he looked over them to see if we could get a closer spot. "I say we go up there." He raised his chin in the air.

I looked up to see where he was pointing.

"I'm up for it." I turned the camera off and put it back in the bag so it didn't get sandy on our way to his lighthouse. The perfect view of the fireworks would be from the tip-top of that structure.

With a touch of excitement lingering in the air, Darren and I climbed the winding staircase from inside his house.

"We better hurry." Darren was ahead of me, holding a six-pack of beer he'd grabbed out of his refrigerator on our way to the steps. "I can hear the booms."

As we reached the top, the vibrant colors of the Fourth of July fireworks painted the night sky above the ocean, creating a breathtaking spectacle.

Darren had a mischievous glint in his eyes as he handed me a couple of chilled beers. Condensation glistened on the bottles. We settled ourselves on the platform, our legs dangling over the side, feeling the cool ocean breeze against our skin.

As the first fireworks exploded above us, we clinked our bottles together in a toast, savoring the fizzy anticipation that mirrored the sparkling lights overhead. The symphony of crackling bursts and whistling trails filled the night, punctuated by gasps and applause from the crowd below.

I couldn't help but feel a sense of awe and gratitude as we sat there, witnessing the colorful bursts of light illuminating the darkness. The waves' rhythmic pounding against the shore added a soothing backdrop to the spectacle, creating a moment of pure enchantment.

"I better snap a few photos." I put my beer bottle down and dragged the bag closer to me.

The photos would be beautiful but nothing like being there in person.

"That should be enough." I wanted to make sure I was present for the rest of photos and satisfied I'd gotten a few good ones to use.

We leaned back against the sturdy structure of the lighthouse, our gazes fixed on the mesmerizing display. Darren's presence beside me brought a warmth and comfort that I had come to cherish while we marveled at the magic unfolding before our eyes.

As the fireworks painted the night sky with cascades of red, white, and blue, the world seemed to fade away, leaving only Darren, the lights, and me. Our laughter and whispered conversations filled the space between the bursts. We shared stories and dreams amidst the symphony of colors.

Time seemed to stand still as we basked in the beauty of the moment. The stars above seemed to twinkle with delight, as if they were joining in the celebration of this special night.

With each explosion, I felt a sense of unity, not only with Darren but also with the entire town of Holiday Junction. It was a moment of collective awe, a shared experience that transcended individual differences and brought us together under the magic of the fireworks.

As the grand finale erupted in a shower of shimmering sparks, we sat in silence, our hearts filled with gratitude and wonder. The sounds of the cheers and applause from the crowd below reached our ears, a testament to the joy and delight the fireworks had brought to everyone in Holiday Junction.

Then some screaming suddenly took over the cheers. Darren and I stood up to see why.

"What's going on?" I asked, leaning over the railing.

As a journalist with an insatiable curiosity, I couldn't help but dart off back down the stairs to get an up-close and personal photo of whatever was going on.

I took a deep breath, allowing the salty breeze to fill my lungs, heightening my senses. The stage was set, the atmosphere charged with anticipation.

Little did I know that by the end of this night, the vibrant celebration would give way to a grim discovery, plunging Holiday Junction into a web of secrets and intrigue.

As soon as we reached the beach, one last burst of fireworks illuminated the darkening sky, and I felt a surge of adrenaline, knowing that my nose for news and the light of the fireworks would lead me straight into the heart of the unfolding mystery.

At the time, I didn't realize it was a dead body on the beach.

CHAPTER TWO

As I pushed my way through the gathering crowd, my heart pounded in my chest once I caught sight of the lifeless body sprawled on the sandy beach. The pale moonlight cast an eerie glow upon his wide, terror-stricken eyes, and the unmistakable marks of strangulation marred his exposed neck. Choked to death, his lifeless form had washed ashore just as the festivities of the Fourth of July had begun.

With a sense of urgency, I instinctively reached for my camera and captured the grim scene in a series of haunting images. Pen and notepad in hand, I meticulously recorded every detail, knowing that this macabre discovery would soon become the town's most haunting tale. Determined to uncover the truth behind this heinous act, I was resolute in my pursuit of justice.

"What are you doing?" Darren had caught up to me.

"I'm getting all of this down. I'm a journalist," I reminded him in an off-putting tone. "I'm sorry, but this is my job."

"Can't you turn it off for one night? There's a dead man, and, well, it just doesn't seem right." Darren's disapproval showed on his face and in those big eyes I'd just been staring into so lovingly.

"Excuse me, excuse me." Chief Matthew Strickland, Darren's father and the Holiday Junction Chief of Police, made his way through the crowd. Louise Strickland—his wife, Darren's mom, and one of the co-owners of the *Junction Journal*—was right behind him.

I turned back to look at Darren, but he wasn't there. He'd left.

"What on earth happened?" Louise asked. Her caftan blew gently from the soft breeze coming off the ocean. The water lapped around our ankles as the tide rushed to shore.

"I don't know." I shook my head. "I do know he was murdered."

"How do you know that?" she asked but kept her eye on her husband, who was on the phone.

Through the chatter and rumbles of the crowd that'd gathered, I could hear Chief Strickland calling for backup.

"Do you see the blood vessel spots around his eyes and on his face?" When she nodded, I explained that petechial hemorrhaging on the face and eyes were a sure sign of strangulation.

"I don't even want to know how you know this," she whispered as the other officers arrived.

Their job appeared to be backing up the crowd, letting them know there was nothing to see here, and encouraging them to go on home because the night's festivities had ended with the fireworks.

That included me.

Even though I tried to see what information I could get from Matthew, I knew he wasn't going to tell me anything and that it would be up to me to get any details. Those would have to wait until the morning because Curtis Robinson, Holiday Junction's coroner, had yet to get there.

"Well?" I asked Louise the loaded one-word question as we made our way up the street along the seaside shops.

"You have a job to do." That was her way of letting me know that the crossing of the fine line between her newspaper and my involvement in a murder investigation her husband was in charge of was full steam ahead.

"And Marge is going to be okay with it?" I had to make sure before I literally plunged full force into finding out what I could about the victim and uncovering any details about why someone would do such a thing.

"She's on board. I can promise you that." Louise gave a little finger wave and got into her golf cart, the preferred method for getting around our small town, other than a bicycle or the trolley. "I'll let you know his name shortly. But I'll see you in the morning for our meeting."

"Shortly" meant that she expected me to go back to the office and see what I could dig up for the morning's news. As for the meeting, it was something she and Marge had told me about this morning. It wasn't scheduled. Not surprising since they never scheduled any meetings.

"See you in the morning," I called, not thinking too much about it. My thoughts were currently racing about the body lying on the beach as I returned to the *Junction Journal* office.

The night's tranquil symphony, the rhythmic crashing of the ocean waves, provided a soundtrack for my swirling thoughts. I couldn't shake the haunting image of the lifeless body from my mind, its presence like a heavy weight upon my shoulders.

The ocean side had gotten deserted fast. The only sounds on-site came from the police on the beach, investigating whatever happened.

Something tugged at my heart when I passed the Jiggle Joint, the bar Darren owned. I called it the Jiggle Joint because it was the kind of establishment where more than Jell-O shots were jigglin', if you knew what I was talking about.

"I'm going in," I said to myself and shoved the door open.

A few minutes would pass before Louise got any information from Matthew, and I had time to go in there to find Darren.

I pushed open the black door, which had no window to peek inside from the sidewalk, and stood still as the door closed behind me, allowing my eyes to adjust to the dark bar and neon light show on the stage.

This performance wasn't the type of show the Jiggle Joint usually had. It was the Mad Fiddlers, the band in which Darren played a mean fiddle.

"If it ain't our spirited reporter." Owen stood up and saluted me. Shawn popped up off the bar stool next to him and placed his hand on his heart.

I'd seen Shawn, the other friendly barfly, sitting next to him, but this was the first time I'd seen Mama sitting next to Shawn.

"It's not like I'm the American flag." I snorted and walked over to Mama. "What are you doing in here?"

"I'm having me a cocktail. Now don't you be going and telling your daddy." She held up the glass and gave it a little shake. The glass's one large ice cube rattled inside it.

Without even asking, I knew what the one big cube meant when it came to Mama—a bourbon old-fashioned. She only drank those when she was stressed, so instead of adding to it, I decided to join her.

I waved my finger in the air at the bartender on duty and got a confirming chin lift.

"When did they go on?" I asked to anyone who would answer and gestured to the Mad Fiddlers.

"It wasn't planned, if that's what you mean." Owen sat back down and picked up his beer bottle. "He came in here a little while ago, and the guys were playing darts."

"Yep. He told them to grab their instruments and get up on stage." Shawn didn't realize he was confirming Darren was mad.

It was a very recognizable action Darren took when he was angry or sad. He turned to music. Currently, I was the reason the band was up there and actually playing really well.

Shoowee.

His stress and Mama's were going to kill me, just like the body that washed up on the beach had been.

Speaking of the body, I knew it was going to be just a matter of time before someone brought it up.

The four of us sat there, sipping on our drinks and enjoying the band. I got a glimpse of Darren looking up at me. Every once in a while, he offered me a faint smile and even a wink.

Though he was anxious about me reporting on the body, his little gestures told me all was good with us. That made me feel so much more relieved.

"What's this I hear about a body?" Owen asked. He took a swig when the band went on a break, giving us enough silence to talk.

"I don't know anything about it." I couldn't take my eyes off Darren.

He really loved playing the fiddle and being part of the band. It was like another world for him. "Who told you?" I asked and watched as Darren changed out some of the strings he'd broken during the last set.

"Body? What dead body?" Mama asked.

"How long have you been in here?" I questioned. "I thought you were giving out your brochures for the Leisure Center."

"Don't you worry about it," Mama muttered.

"Darren was mumbling something about it when he came in, and, well, you are the Lois Lane to the Easter Bunny and Tooth Fairy." Shawn gestured between him and Owen with his beer bottle, and then they clinked their bottles together.

When I first met them, that was how they introduced themselves to me. Owen claimed he was the Easter Bunny. He did try out for that part during Easter but sadly didn't get it. Shawn teased me that he was the Tooth Fairy.

I had a mind like an elephant's and never forgot anything, which was how I not only referred to them but also introduced them.

"I see there's a few tourists in here tonight." I was impressed since most nights the Jiggle Joint had only one or two other customers other than the barflies, Owen, and Shawn.

"That guy has been here a few nights." Owen pointed the bottle at the lone man at the corner table.

"Huh." My eyes lowered as I tried to get a good look at him, but the bar was so dark I could only make out a shadowy outline. "Tell Darren to call me, please."

"Will do." Owen swiveled the barstool around to face me.

"Where are you going?" Mama asked and took out a few dollars from her purse. She set them on top of the bar and used the cup as a paperweight.

"I've got to go see what's up with that body for the morning paper." After all, I was the only real employee the *Junction Journal* had. Mama was an employee, too, but she didn't do any writing, though she was instrumental in the research department. She was good at that.

"All the meddlin' around" was what Daddy said made Mama good. She claimed she'd never meddled. "It's not meddlin' if someone is telling you and you never asked them to"—according to her.

Mama had her own reasoning, which was fine with me. That was what made her good for the paper.

When I started working for Louise and Marge, the paper was in dire need of resuscitation. With a lot of coaxing, I was able to get them to move the *Junction Journal* office from their home compound in downtown Holiday Junction to the cute cottage their nephew, Rhett Strickland, owned on the town's coast.

That way, I could come and go as I needed to, and tonight was definitely going to be a long one as I waited for Louise to tell me the name of the victim of the brutal crime.

"I'm coming with you." Mama got up and said her goodbyes to the Tooth Fairy and Easter Bunny.

On our way back to the office, I sorted through my mind about the man on the beach, trying to make sense of the chaos surrounding the murder. Mama must've been deep in thought, too, because she didn't utter a word.

My mind buzzed with questions, each one a puzzle piece yearning to be fitted together. Who was that man? What drove someone to commit such a heinous act on a night meant for celebration?

The answers eluded me, but my determination burned bright, fueled by a thirst for truth and justice, even if Darren wasn't happy with how I'd handled my response. He would play his emotions out tonight, and I was confident that by the morning, he'd calm down enough for us to have a reasonable conversation.

I had to put all of that in the back of my head. In journalism, you had to take any and all emotions out of the task at hand, and right now,

I had to get the article written. After all, it could be picked up by the Associated Press, and that would be great for my career.

I hurriedly made my way down the street and up the dunes toward the office, my mind filled with the pressing urgency of what investigation I might have to do tomorrow.

My phone chirped before I could get my key into the lock of the office door.

"If that's your daddy, tell him I'm working," Mama said, making me wonder if something was going on between them. It wasn't like they'd been exempt from marital troubles.

In fact, when Mama showed up on Mother's Day a year ago, she'd informed me she and Daddy were getting a divorce. She was going to leave him and live with me.

I didn't get into too much of their little spat because that was just what they did. They fussed and argued, threatening to leave each other, and then they'd be playing kissy-face in the crook of the kitchen counter where the lazy Susan was located.

Nor did I want to get into the middle of their shenanigans.

"It's Louise. She said she got a look at Matthew's notes and the body belongs to Graham Winston." I unlocked the door and turned on the lights as soon as we stepped inside.

"The local art dealer?" Mama asked.

"I don't know. How do you know?" I questioned and headed into my office, leaving her to shut the door behind her.

"The Leisure Center has an art studio, and I thought it would be fun to gather some local art and hire Cassandra Firbank to teach a class a week or something. You know old people." Mama lumped all elderly folks into the same category. "They love to paint."

"They do?" My brow rose at her assumption.

"Don't be yelling at me in that tone," she warned. "I know you don't think we like to do things, but we like to paint."

"I didn't say you did, but I don't think all elderly people like to paint." I flipped open my laptop on the desk. As I waited for it to come to life, I walked over to the big whiteboard Mama and I used to plan out the various articles about the weekly recurring events.

Like funeral notices, houses for sale, items for sale, help wanted—you know, things that we'd get calls on. Instead of writing these events down on paper, we just went ahead and wrote them on the board so they could sit in front of me as I prepared the paper for publication.

"What do you know about him?" I asked Mama, erasing all the events on the board to make room for our murder investigation.

Mama sat down at my desk and tapped away, bringing up everything she could find on the internet about him. As she rattled the information off, I used the dry-erase marker to write down anything and everything she was saying, even if it was something like the victim having a cat. Nothing was too insignificant when researching a murder and writing an article about it.

It was the smallest of details that brought a killer out. Heck, if Graham had a cat, maybe the veterinarian killed him over something weird. Who knew?

But Mama and I were going to find out as much as we could.

After all, we were the *Junction Journal*.

"Graham Winston is fifty-two years old. He's the owner of Winston's Art Emporium located downtown." Mama continued to read off the screen, the light glowing on her face. "Over the years, he earned a reputation for having a keen eye for undiscovered talent and bringing unique pieces to the town's art enthusiasts. Though a private man, Graham enjoyed the small-town life and attended the community events that brought everyone together."

"Wow," I said with a little shock. "Are you writing his obituary already?" I asked. She did write a lot of them for the *Junction Journal* if the family didn't turn anything in for the notification in the obituary section.

"I'm reading an article from the *Junction Journal* a few years ago where he was a featured business owner in the town. That's a really good idea," Mama said.

"What is?" I asked and walked over to see what she was eyeballing.

"Featured section with a business. We should start that back up." She used her finger to move the laptop's mouse pointer to the section header. "The Leisure Center could be our first one."

"Oh, I see." I laughed, knowing she'd taken the angle to work for her, which was pretty smart. "Let's stick to finding out what we can about Graham and table the discussion about the new feature until tomorrow, when we have our meeting with the sisters."

"I forgot about that." Mama sighed and went back to reading the facts she found online about Graham.

I went back to writing those down. The whiz of the printer made me pause.

Mama reached down, plucked off the paper, and held it out for me.

"Graham was a tall, distinguished-looking man with salt-and-pepper hair and a warm, captivating smile." Mama's words dripped with interest. "According to this article, he was known for his impeccable taste in clothes and had an air of sophistication about him. He lived alone in a cozy cottage near the beach and took great pride in his small but lush garden. He was known to be an excellent cook, often hosting intimate dinner parties for his close friends, where they would enjoy fine food, wine, and conversations about art and culture."

"My goodness. He sounds like a catch. What about a wife and kids?" I asked, trying to get Mama's eyes off the poor dead man's photo, which she'd printed to tape up on the murder board.

"Graham was unmarried and had no children," Mama continued to read. "'Once I was engaged to my high school sweetheart, but we decided to go our separate ways when I decided to travel the world for art. She's a hometown gal with a heart of gold. It was best she lived in Holiday Junction while I traveled the world.'"

"Oh." My brows shot up, and I wrote the word "girlfriend" with a big asterisk beside it on the murder board. "If we can find out who she is, maybe she still lives here. She would know him best. After all, they almost got engaged."

"Someone wrote something about him about being a shady art dealer." Mama hit on something with that. "Now, that would give someone a motive."

"What does it say?" I asked, making another bullet point under the list of suspects and writing "possible shady art deal" as a motive.

"While Graham's professional success was undeniable, there were whispers about some underhanded dealings in the art world that he might have been involved in. Some believed that he had a secret network of smugglers and thieves who supplied him with stolen or counterfeit art pieces. Others speculated that he used his gallery as a front for money laundering." Mama's voice faded away as she glanced up over the screen at me. "*Art Dealer* magazine from three years ago."

"Three years ago?" I questioned the timing, but it was still something to look at, especially if he used his shop here to do the laundering.

"Mm-hmm, about the time he bought the property from Joaquin Camsen after another deal on a piece of property had fallen through." Mama's brow peaked.

"It looks like we need to stop by and see Joaquin Camsen tomorrow." I knew the only realtor in town very well, and so did Mama.

"Mm-hmm and possibly Layla." Mama referred to Joaquin's wife, the village's busybody.

In just a few minutes, Mama and I had filled out the next day's calendar to make a few stops to inquire about Graham and why someone would want to kill him, let alone strangle him.

After all, that he had been strangled suggested that his killer harbored a deep personal animosity toward him. And I just couldn't let that little bit of journalistic curiosity be a snippet in the newspaper.

There was something much more sinister to this murder, and I was going to learn all the details.

CHAPTER THREE

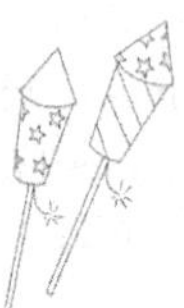

There was no need for me to set an alarm. I couldn't sleep, and no shops were open in the middle of the night, so I decided to get dressed and walk to the office.

Yes, there was a killer on the loose, but I didn't think it was the serial kind. There did seem to be reasons for someone who wouldn't otherwise kill anyone to want to murder him.

Under the moonlight's gentle glow, I found myself walking through Holiday Park in the stillness of the night. The warm summer air caressed my skin, carrying with it the anticipation of the upcoming Fourth of July festivities. As I strolled along the path, my steps echoing softly, I marveled at the transformation that awaited this vibrant park with the break of dawn.

The park, usually a tranquil oasis, would soon come alive with activity. The large fountain at its center, dormant for now, would become the focal point of the Parade Extravaganza. I imagined the joyous cheers and laughter that would fill the air as the parade route concluded at the fountain, its cascading waters adding a touch of whimsy to the celebratory scene.

Fern Banks, the local beauty queen, would smile as the young girls ran up to her for her autograph. That would definitely be a photo I had to take. I'd already gotten several text messages from Fern to confirm and reconfirm I'd be there.

Passing by the lake, I saw the shimmering reflections of colorful vendor booths as they were lined up to open to the tourists and locals. I imagined the aroma of mouthwatering treats and the buzz of excited chatter intertwining, creating an atmosphere of festive anticipation.

Yet, despite the vibrancy that lay just a few hours away, my thoughts were still consumed by the lingering murder that had cast a dark shadow over the town. That death had just taken place a few hours ago and robbed me of getting any sleep.

The memory of the lifeless body on the beach haunted my mind, a chilling reminder that danger could lurk in the most idyllic of settings.

A rustling sound nearby jolted me out of my reverie, making my heart skip a beat. Instinctively, I reached into my bag, and my fingers closed around the comforting presence of my Mace. Adrenaline coursed through my veins as I cautiously approached the source of the noise.

"You almost got maced," I told the harmless nighttime critter scurrying through the bushes, seeking its own nocturnal adventures.

Chuckling at my overactive imagination, I continued on the path leading down to the beach, the sound of crashing waves growing louder with each step. The lighthouse stood tall and proud. The beacon atop it rolled around, giving me even more light the closer I got to the beach.

The sight that greeted me at the shoreline was breathtaking. The moon cast a shimmering trail upon the glistening waves, turning the vast expanse of water into a silver tapestry. Above, the starry sky provided a celestial backdrop to this serene nighttime scene.

As I stood there, caught between the serenity of the beach and the echoes of the unsettling crime that had unfolded in these very waters, I felt a renewed determination.

I would not let fear cloud my pursuit of the truth. Graham deserved justice, and the town deserved to be free from the grip of darkness.

Taking a deep breath, I allowed the beauty of the night to wash over me, grounding me in the present moment. With each inhale, I drew strength from the lapping of the waves and the shimmer of the moon. They reminded me that even amidst turmoil and uncertainty, the world still held moments of tranquility and hope.

Closing my eyes, I whispered a silent promise to the victims and to myself that I would not rest until the truth was uncovered. With the lingering scent of the sea and the echoes of the night guiding my steps, I turned back toward the town, ready to face the challenges that lay ahead.

The journalistic instinct in me had to get to the truth. What had happened? Why would someone kill him with such a force of strangulation?

As more and more questions piled up, I was standing in front of the office cottage.

When I stepped up on the first stair, I caught sight of a peculiar figure through the window.

A shadowy silhouette moved about inside, rummaging through the papers on my desk. I furrowed my brow, my heart pounding with a mix of concern and curiosity.

Instinctively, I reached into the camera bag and retrieved the trusty canister of Mace I kept for emergencies. With a firm grip on the canister, I took a deep breath to steady myself, ready to confront the intruder head-on.

My adrenaline pumping, I burst through the door, bolted into my office, and aimed the Mace at the unsuspecting figure.

But to my surprise, what escaped my lips was not a cry of alarm but a startled squeak as the Mace accidentally sprayed across the room, enveloping both the intruder and me in its spicy cloud.

"Hold it right there! My boyfriend's father is the police chief, and he's on his way!" I lied as I coughed and sputtered.

"Stop! Stop!" the man screamed, also through his own fit of barking and hacking.

"No!" I jabbed the canister toward him and pressed down. Nothing came out, so I threw it at him. "I will not let you steal anything!"

I finally managed to regain my composure. My eyes were now fixed on the man who stood before me, blinking away the effects of the Mace.

He was slightly older, with a disheveled but endearing charm about him. A mix of embarrassment and amusement danced in his eyes as he held up a key and a driver's license.

"I swear I'm not a burglar! My name is Radley, and I'm the new journalist Marge Strickland hired," he explained, his voice tinged with a touch of laughter. "I was just trying to find a file I needed, but I think I stumbled upon the wrong desk."

"New journalist?" I blinked, feeling the burn of the Mace linger. "What are you talking about? I don't know anything about a new journalist. I'm the journalist."

"Are you Violet or Millie Kay?" he asked.

"I'm Violet Rhinehammer." I stood tall and tried to glare at him through my watery eyes.

"You're the editor in chief, Violet Rhinehammer?" He tugged the edges of his shirt up to his eyes, exposing his very toned set of abs. "I'm a journalist."

"What are you talking about?" I asked.

"Marge and I go way back." He went to stick his hand in his pocket. "I'm just taking out my phone to show you the text she sent me."

He turned the phone around and showed me a text in which Marge had told him to come to the office.

"It says tomorrow, but I got in a little earlier than I expected, so I thought I'd just come to the office and sleep here until I can get to the Jubilee Inn. Marge has me booked there until I can find a place."

"Place? Job?" I questioned.

"She didn't tell you, did she?" he asked.

"No, she didn't." I shook my head.

"I'm sorry. Marge just does things and doesn't think too much about them." He snorted. "She's always been that way."

"There is a meeting in the morning, and I'm guessing it's about you joining the team." Now I understood what the unusual meeting was going to be about.

"Here, I'll shoot her a text to let her know I'm in town early." He started to tap on his phone.

"That's okay." I shook my head. "There's a pull-out couch in Mama's office, and you'll find some sheets and covers in the small closet in there as well as some pillows. We like to keep things stocked in case we do have to spend the night. Plus, there's a full kitchen in the back, so you can make coffee in the morning. I doubt there's anything good to eat, but I can bring you something."

My cheeks flushed, and I couldn't help but feel a mixture of relief and mirth at the absurdity of the situation. I carefully set the Mace aside, making a mental note to apologize to the intruder, now revealed to be Radley, for my mistaken assumption.

"Radley, huh? Sorry about the whole Mace mishap," I stammered, my voice laced with both amusement and embarrassment. "Welcome to the Junction Journal."

Radley chuckled, his laughter contagious as it filled the room. "Well, Violet, it's certainly been quite the memorable introduction. And hey, at least we know the Mace works, right?"

I couldn't help but smile, realizing that this unexpected encounter had turned into a lighthearted and funny moment. As we stumbled over each other's words, trying to regain our composure, Radley tossed the key and driver's license onto the desk.

"Here's the key to the office cottage and my license, just to prove that I'm not here to cause trouble," he said, a playful twinkle in his eyes.

With a laugh, I reached over and grabbed the key, examining it briefly. "All right, Radley, I believe you. Welcome to the team. Let's hope our future encounters are a little less... spicy. How do you know Marge?"

"She and my dad dated when I was a kid." He threw me off with that one, and I didn't explore it anymore.

As we awkwardly stumbled over our words, still chuckling at the absurdity of the situation, I couldn't help but feel a sense of excitement for the unexpected twists and turns that awaited us both at the *Junction Journal*.

He seemed like a nice guy. I wasn't sure of his age, but he definitely wasn't older like I'd initially thought. With time, I figured we would know all about each other.

"What's the big scoop around here besides all the fireworks and stuff?" he asked.

"A body washed up on the beach tonight."

"A body, huh?" he asked. The color came back to his face.

"Murdered dead body," I said and watched his face light up even more.

"Just the kinda thing I like. What's his name?" Radley walked over to the big whiteboard in my office and picked up the dry eraser. "Do you mind?" he asked, referring to wiping off the board.

"Not at all." I was curious to see what he was going to do. "We don't have a name or any information on him yet. It just happened. That's why I'm here. I was going to write up a quick article for the morning edition and go through my photos."

"I can do that." Radley put the eraser down. "Why don't you go on home. Get some shut-eye, maybe wash your eyes out from the Mace, and come back in the morning with fresh eyes."

"You don't need to do my job." I laughed and wondered what our roles were.

"Really. I don't mind. I've got nothing to do tonight anyways since I'm sure I'll be up all night from the long airplane ride and car ride here. I can go through the photos. I'm pretty good at digital imaging, so it's not a big deal." He picked up the camera bag and unzipped it. "Nice. I've used one of these before. I'll write something up, and you can look at it in the morning. If you like it, you can change it or toss it out."

I hesitated.

"That's why I'm here. To help you out." He shooed me to the door. "See you in the morning."

"No." I twisted around. "I'm staying."

No way was I going to leave this Radley feller here by himself.

"I'll just call Marge." I took my phone out and woke up a sleepy boss who did, in fact, confirm Radley's new job but also muttered a few curse words about him showing up early. Then the boss cursed his father, which I didn't mention to Radley.

"And Violet," Marge muttered. "The victim on beach is named Graham Winston."

Graham Winston, I said in my head to remember the name.

"Are we good?" Radley asked after I hung up the phone. "You can go home now."

"Don't touch my board," I instructed him. "That's mine. We will figure out what's yours in the morning. Oh." I turned back when I started to walk out. "The victim on the beach is Graham Winston."

We were going to be figuring out more than that, but that's what I left him with.

CHAPTER FOUR

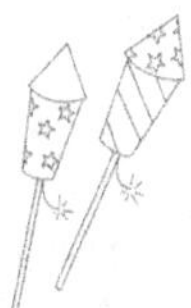

Mama was up bright and early with a smile on her face and a southern drawl telling me, "Get up—we have some investigatin' to do."

"I did me a little research while you were getting your beauty sleep." Mama took a left off Heart Street, where we currently lived.

No. I didn't live with my parents. Yes, I did live in the garage in their backyard, but in my defense, I paid rent.

The golf cart whizzed down the main street. The wind felt good on this very early summer morning. The sunrise was now around six thirty a.m. The time was seven thirty, so the sun was already up high in the sky.

"Didn't you get any beauty sleep?" I asked and held on for dear life when Mama got a little too close to the bumper of a car. Just then, she whipped the cart into the parking spot designated for golf carts in front of Brewing Beans.

I hadn't let her in on the new employee, Radley what's-his-name. Did I even get his last name? I couldn't recall, but I did know that Mama was going to find him very interesting. And I knew Mama would interrogate him better than any lawyer or officer of the law. I'd never seen anything like it. Mama had no filter when it came to getting into people's personal business upon meeting them, and Radley would be one I couldn't wait for. Especially after his little bombshell about how he knew Marge.

"I'm not concerned with my beauty. It's you I'm worried about," Mama said with a *tsk*. I knew better than to leave the door wide open when it came to anything about beauty and my age. "You're rounding to thirty, and, well, let me tell you, when I was thirty, I was baking cupcakes for your third birthday."

"Mama." I sighed.

"I know, Violet." She bent down, put the golf cart into park, and turned it off. "Things are different these days. What is so wrong with the older days?"

"Who am I going to marry?" I asked and got out to meet her on the sidewalk.

"I reckon Darren Strickland. It ain't like he don't already take the privilege of sneaking through our gate at midnight." Mama stood in front of the coffee shop door, which she did not have to tell me to open for her.

It was the southern way of holding the door open for your elders, and she expected it.

Even Darren didn't get exempt from Mama's rules on manners. We'd gone out to supper one night, and Mama stood at the door for what felt like an eternity until Darren got the hint she wasn't opening her own door.

While she had us at the table that night, she spent the entire supper giving Darren southern gentleman lessons, and he still stuck around. I was thinking he was a keeper, but it was all still very early in the relationship and only recently had gone public, so no engagement ring was ever discussed.

Once we did start to do things around the village and held hands where people noticed, Mama had practically planned my wedding.

"We are dating. That's it." I shook my head and headed up to the counter, where Hershal and Hazelynn Hudson had already gotten our to-go coffees and a box of their fresh orange scones ready for us.

"What do you know about the murder?" Hazelynn asked. "I know you're in here too early to just be going to work."

"And we've gotten really good at seeing how you do things when there's a dead body." Hershal gleamed. He was an even bigger gossip than his wife, but they were harmless.

"Maybe it was an art deal gone bad," Mama chirped.

"Art deal?" Hazelynn's mouth dropped. "Victor Monroe?" she cried out and brought her hand to her mouth. "I should've reported the fight between him and Graham Winston that day." She shook a finger at Hershal. "I told you I should've called Chief Strickland."

"Victor Monroe?" Mama jerked back. "No. The victim is Graham Winston."

"Graham?" Hazelynn cried out again, this time loudly enough for some of the customers sitting at the tables inside the coffee shop to turn around to see what the hubbub was about.

"Shhh." I nudged Mama and handed her one of the coffees. "We aren't really sure of all the details."

"We know it's Graham Winston who was strangled to death." Mama picked up the box of scones.

"Strangled?" Hazelynn lifted her hands to her neck as if she could feel what had happened.

"We don't know." I shook my head. "Mama, I'll meet you out in the golf cart."

"Violet—" Mama started to protest. "All right. Fine." She turned on a dime and shimmied across the coffee shop, giving little hellos and how-are-yous to people she recognized. "Y'all, don't forget about the new Leisure Center," she hollered as she waited for the customer coming inside to hold open the door for her.

"Now what's this business about Victor Monroe and Graham Winston having a public argument?" I asked, turning back to Hazelynn.

"Go on, Hershal. It's your turn." She shooed him off to the kitchen. "We take turns putting things in the ovens and making the coffee. It's his turn, but he wants to sit right here and listen to what we have to say."

I snickered. The two had been married a long time.

"Anyways, the other day they were in here at the same time, and well, if you know anything about their long-standing feud about this art gallery business..." She rolled her eyes. "I wouldn't know a Monet from Mona down the road. But those two, they got that eye, and when a painting either of them wants for his gallery comes up, they fuss and fight over who is going to win. And it turned ugly over the last one."

"How so?" I asked and took a few dollar bills out of my purse to give her for the coffee and scones.

"Victor accused Graham of a forgery. And by the way they were arguing, that's one of the worst things you can do as an art dealer." She took the cash from me and haphazardly counted it before shoving it in the cash drawer.

"Do you remember what painting Victor was talking about?" I asked.

"No. Like I said, I wouldn't know a thing about paintings." She shook her head. "You see that over there on the wall?"

She pointed at the picture I'd seen a million times.

"When Graham opened his art gallery, which—don't get me started on that incident..." Hazelynn frowned. "He didn't have a place to store some of his pieces and asked if he could do it here. Brewing Beans looked more like an art gallery than a coffee shop. He said we could keep that one on loan because it looked so pretty there."

"That was nice of him." I'd noticed the landscape painting many times when I came in for coffee. It showed a small beach town that was similar to Holiday Junction but didn't have the mountains on the far side of town. The painting included a lighthouse like the one where Darren lived.

"Yeah. He said it wasn't worth much, but he felt like it went with the village." She shrugged. "I guess I'll have to let Diffy Delk know it's here in case it's in Graham's will."

"Diffy Delk?" I asked, knowing she meant one of the local lawyers in the village.

"Yep. He financed Graham's first gallery showing."

Hazelynn made no sense to me, which told me I didn't know enough about the art world and had a little homework to do before I could really investigate.

"What about Emily?" she asked.

"Emily?" Hazelynn was throwing out so many names, I was about to take my phone out and start typing them in my Notes app.

"Graham's assistant. Poor girl. I guess she won't have a job." Hazelynn glanced up when one of the baristas called for her. "I've got to go. Poor Graham."

"Victor, Emily, Diffy," I repeated the entire way back to the office.

Hazelynn's intriguing tidbits about Graham sparked a fire within me, igniting my journalistic instincts and sending my mind into overdrive.

As the golf cart bumped along the dirt path, I mentally sifted through the possible motives that Victor could have had for accusing Graham. Jealousy, rivalry, or even a personal vendetta against him—all these scenarios danced in my mind, each one a thread to unravel in my quest for the truth.

My plan crystallized as I mulled over the next steps in the investigation. I would pay a visit to Victor in his art gallery, seeking answers and insight into his accusations against Graham of forgery. Perhaps he held valuable information that could shed light on Graham's potential involvement in the forgery. I made a mental note to approach the meeting with cautious determination, ready to use my investigative skills to their fullest.

But Victor wasn't the only piece in this intricate puzzle. Hazelynn had also mentioned that Graham's assistant, Emily, held her own set of secrets.

A conversation with her might reveal a deeper understanding of Graham's artistic practices and shed light on any questionable activities. I would need to tread carefully, delicately coaxing information while protecting my sources.

The golf cart rolled to a gentle stop in front of the *Junction Journal*'s seaside cottage office, the sunlight casting a warm glow on the weathered facade.

"You ready to get this day started?" Mama hopped out and hurried up the sidewalk leading to the small porch of the office. She used her key to get in before I even got halfway to the cottage.

Granted, I'd looked down the seaside toward the lighthouse, hoping to catch a glimpse of Darren possibly walking out of it. In reality, though, it was much too early for him to open his eyes for the day.

"Who are you?" Mama yelled.

Yep. She'd met Radley.

"I carry a gun! You stay right there! I'm calling the poe-leece!" Mama's accent was deeper when she was excited or scared.

"Mama, don't be going and calling nobody." I came in to find Radley with his hands in the air and a frightened look on his face. "And Mama doesn't pack any guns. Put your hands down."

"Radley who? Radley what? As in what do you want?" Mama put her hands on her hips.

"I've been looking at this information you gave me about the man washed up on the beach last night." Radley went right on into what he'd been up to all night, judging by his disheveled clothes and the bags under his eyes, searching on the internet. "And he's had a real shady past."

"Why have you been looking up information?" Mama asked. Suddenly, her eyes popped wide open as if she just discovered something huge. "Oh my geezer! You're with the FBI!"

"FBI?" Radley asked. "No, ma'am, I'm with the *Junction Journal*. At least as of this morning after the meeting. I got into town earlier than expected, and since my room at the Jubilee Inn won't be ready, I just stayed here last night but couldn't sleep, so I worked."

"Employee?" Mama's face went back to being confused. "There's only two employees here at this office. That's me and Violet."

"You're Millie Kay." Amusement shone in his eyes and then proceeded to reach his lips. "I heard about you."

"From who?" Mama jerked up and pulled on the hem of her white button-down. "I demand to know who and what they said."

"Now I can't tell all my secrets. I'm a journalist." He winked.

"I will find out." Mama put the box of scones on the desk. "We brought scones today. Tomorrow you can bring something. Good to have someone else to carry the load around here."

Mama took a seat at my desk and made herself a little breakfast plate while I sipped my coffee and looked at the murder board we'd started, to which Radley had added. There was a definite distinction between his handwriting and mine.

"Each one of them is involved with Graham. They all have some sort of relationship that would paint us a picture of what type of businessman he was, client for Diffy and boss for Emily," I noted once we got back into the office.

Mama got up from the seat and opened the window to let the coastal breeze carrying the scent of salt and adventure flutter throughout the cottage. While she did that, Radley went over what he'd found out on the internet, all of which I'd already discovered. I filled him in on what Hazelynn had told me this morning.

The warm July morning was just beginning, and I was ready to dive deeper into the shadows of Holiday Junction, armed with my curiosity and the unwavering pursuit of truth to see just who could do such a thing to Graham.

"What on earth are you going to put into this morning's edition? It's set to go out in about ten minutes." Mama was referring to the online daily version of the *Junction Journal*. "I don't see a public notice on here."

She was talking about the police department giving a statement to put into the paper, which told me something.

"They've not let the public know it was Graham Winston yet. That's why I told you not to say anything at Brewing Beans." I quickly wrote down Victor Monroe under the suspect list and added a couple of bullet points about an argument over a possible forgery.

"You didn't tell me not to say anything. You just rudely interrupted me." Mama was going to turn it around on me somehow. "I reckon we can just hit publish on what you already did for today's Fourth of July festivities."

"There's our bosses." I pointed out the window.

It was just best to let her think she was right instead of fuss with her about it. I had better things to do.

Louise and Marge had pulled up in their fancy car. As they walked up, I waved out the open window.

"The door's open," I said so they didn't have to worry about fiddling with a key.

"Matthew is going to be so mad." Marge rubbed her hands together in anticipation of what her brother would think after she noticed the murder board. "But we've got a paper to put out, and that's exactly what we hired you to do."

"That's right. You know..." Louise waltzed into the room, her caftan fluttering behind her. It rested at her shins after she stopped in front of the board. "I think Matthew wanted the *Junction Journal* to fail because of these situations." Louise stopped talking and looked at Radley. "Who are you?"

"This is Radley Jordon." Marge barged in and rushed over, making hand gestures in front of him like we were trying to win him on *The Price Is Right*. "I told you we needed another journalist because we are growing so much Violet needs help."

"What am I?" Mama asked. "An old shoe?"

"Now, Millie Kay," Marge said, speaking for herself and Louise, "we know you want to make the Leisure Center a huge hit, and we think it's going to be. That will tie your hands up and leave Violet here with no help."

"I will always help my daughter," Mama stated matter-of-factly. "But you are right about one thing, and that's how the Leisure Center is going to be even bigger than huge." She picked up the box of scones and offered it to Marge and Louise. "Now let's talk about what Matthew's panties are going to be in a wad about. The murdery kinda investigations?"

"Yes. He thought just because we are family, it means we will just skip right over the bad things happening in Holiday Junction," Marge called out behind her as she proceeded down the hall to the kitchen. "No coffee?"

Louise kept her eye on Radley the entire time, but Marge just acted as if he'd been part of the team since day one.

"We just got here and stopped by Brewing Beans, which I'm glad we did because now I have three people to interview." I finished writing down Emily's name as a character witness and Diffy Delk's.

"What is with Joaquin?" Louise picked at the edges of the scone before delicately putting the piece in her mouth.

Out of the corner of my eye, I saw Radley was taking notes. I admired him for that.

"I'm going to go see him about Graham's studio and who sold it to Graham," Mama said.

If Mama did that, then I would have even more time to go see Victor and possibly Emily.

"I still need to cover some of the Fourth of July festivities." I set the dry-erase marker down and picked up the Holiday Junction brochure. "I certainly can't miss the Parade Extravaganza this morning. I can't be doing several things at once."

Today's activities would be kicked off with a vibrant, spirited parade winding its way through the streets of Holiday Junction.

Colorful floats, marching bands, and community groups would be decked out in red, white, and blue to showcase their creativity and enthusiasm. I wanted to have a float for the *Junction Journal,* but the Stricklands said we didn't have it in the budget, and well, since there was one journalist and one photographer—me—I had to do it all.

"Let him do that." Louise pointed the end of her scone at Radley and then popped it into her mouth.

"I'll be more than happy to get out of this office and walk around. Check-in isn't until three o'clock, so I've got plenty of time." Radley tucked in his shirttails, which made him start to look like he did when I first met him.

"Violet, why don't you take Radley to the Jubilee Inn and see if Kristine can get him in a little earlier?" Marge suggested.

"Sure." I shrugged and glanced up at the trolley schedule. "We can catch the trolley in about ten minutes."

"Why the trolley?" Louise asked. "Don't you want to walk down the seaside, past the lighthouse, and up the path to Holiday Park, where the parade route ends?"

The tone of her voice told me she wanted to make sure Darren was still at the forefront of my mind and heart.

"I think the trolley is part of Holiday Junction, and it's a great experience for your first full day here," Marge injected.

"I was thinking Goldie Bennett could give him a little rundown of the village like she gave me the first time I got on the trolley. It was very beneficial information for a transplant." I had not even thought about Darren, but by the way Louise was acting and treating Marge, I knew she had something else on her mind.

"Be sure to let him know you've got a boyfriend," Mama blurted out because she, too, could sense what Louise was saying. "And it's your boss's son." Mama wasn't about to leave out the most important detail.

"That's good because I've got a girlfriend." Radley had put all the moms in the room at ease.

"Grab the camera bag and let's go," I told him. We excused ourselves from the informal meeting that never was. Or was it that Marge was there strictly to introduce Radley to Louise? I didn't know.

The only thing I knew and appreciated was that he was here to help me. If he covered all the candid photos of the parade, I'd be able to stop by Winston Art Gallery since they were on the list of shops that would be open during the Fourth of July week of festivities.

If they happened to close due to the circumstances, I'd bet the employees would talk about it.

Ding, ding. The cling of the trolley bell echoed just before we saw the small vehicle for getting around the village, helmed by Goldie Bennett.

As the trolley rattled along the picturesque streets of Holiday Junction, the morning sun cast a golden glow upon the town. I sat beside Radley.

Goldie was a true embodiment of the Fourth of July spirit. She'd done what she did for every holiday, but it was pure enjoyment to see Radley's face when he looked at her.

Her outfit was a vibrant expression of patriotism, reflecting her love for the holiday. She wore a flowing skirt adorned with stars and stripes, paired with a bright-red blouse that perfectly matched her infectious energy. Goldie accessorized with an assortment of jewelry, each piece intricately designed to evoke the patriotic colors and symbols of the nation. Her earrings dangled like miniature fireworks, and her bold necklace showcased a pendant shaped like the American flag.

Goldie's fiery spirit was matched by her deep knowledge of the town's history. She had witnessed decades of Fourth of July celebrations and eagerly shared her wisdom with anyone who boarded her trolley. Her stories were blends of fact and folklore, keeping the town's heritage alive in its residents' hearts.

It wasn't long before she noticed Radley was from outside the village, and since he was with me, she assumed he was a relative.

"I bet Millie Kay is going to have a big hoedown." Goldie dragged her chin sideways to get a glance before she peeked up in the large mirror above her head. "A hoedown is what you call it back in Kentucky, right?"

"At the Leisure Center?" I asked and shrugged. "Who knows what she's got going on down there."

"No, since your..." Goldie searched for what to call Radley.

"Radley?" I laughed. "Oh no. He's a new employee of the *Junction Journal*, and I know you tell a lot of history about the village as you drive, so I thought it would be great to jump on."

The gorgeous morning unfolded before us like a painting. The sky was an expanse of brilliant blue, adorned with fluffy white clouds that seemed to dance in the gentle breeze. The scent of freshly cut grass mingled with the sweet aroma of blooming flowers, permeating the air with the essence of summer.

Goldie, with her feisty demeanor and deep knowledge of the town's history, regaled us with tales of Holiday Junction's past as the trolley chugged along. She spoke passionately about the Merry Maker, the mysterious figure responsible for spreading merriment and organizing the town's festivities. She revealed that the grand finale of the week-long holiday events, an enchanting affair that the Merry Maker had meticulously planned, would be held on the beach.

Curiosity brimming in his eyes, Radley leaned forward, his interest piqued. "Who could this Merry Maker be? It sounds like quite the secret identity."

I gave Radley a knowing glance, realizing the delicate balance we needed to maintain. I couldn't let him know that Darren and I were the ones behind the Merry Maker's mask. It was a cherished secret held by a select few in the village, and revealing it would shatter the magic that the Merry Maker had woven for years.

I placed a hand on Radley's arm, my voice soft but firm. "Radley, the identity of the Merry Maker is a well-guarded secret here. It's an integral part of the village's charm and traditions. We must respect the anonymity and let the Merry Maker continue their work undisturbed."

Goldie chimed in, her eyes sparkling with mischief. "Oh, don't you worry, darlings. The Merry Maker has been a mystery for as long as I can remember. We all love the surprises and the joy they bring. They're part of what makes our little village so special."

Goldie's attention then turned to Radley, scanning him curiously. "So, Radley, where are you from? You don't seem like a local boy. And do you have a girlfriend? I don't see a ring on that finger of yours."

Radley chuckled, adjusting his collar nervously. "I'm originally from a small town upstate. As for the girlfriend, well, I'm currently enjoying the single life. Came here for a fresh start, you know? Marge actually offered me the job at the *Junction Journal*. I knew her from way back when. Small world, isn't it?"

Goldie's eyes widened, and she wore a surprised expression that seemed frozen in time as we pulled up to our stop—the Jubilee Inn. I couldn't help but smile at the sight, knowing that Radley's connection to Marge had caught her off guard.

"What does that mean?" Goldie asked. "Way back?"

"She and my dad dated for a while." Goldie slammed on the brakes right in front of the Jubilee Inn. She muttered under her breath, "Well, I'll be. What a small world indeed."

I stood up, signaling to Radley that we'd reached our stop. He joined me. We had to wait a couple of seconds before Goldie swung the lever, opening the doors to let us off.

Her mind was churning about Marge and Radley's father. As far as I knew and from what I gathered from the village folks, Marge had always been single and never mingled. But with Radley here, it seemed she had another side we didn't know.

Unlike Radley, who wanted to investigate and reveal who the Merry Maker might be, I wanted to know about his father and Marge.

With a final wave, Radley and I disembarked from the trolley, leaving Goldie with a mix of astonishment and intrigue.

"She's very colorful." He stood on the sidewalk, watching Goldie continue straight right before she made a sharp U-turn because the main street dead-ended into Holiday Park.

"She sure is, and she has a good heart too." I sighed and turned to the front of the Jubilee Inn. A long line wrapped around the building.

"Are all these people wanting a room in that small inn?" he asked.

"No." I laughed and motioned for Radley to follow me, leading him to a clearing where an adorable Boston terrier named Paisley held court.

Paisley, with her sleek black-and-white coat, wore an outfit befitting her esteemed title as the village mayor. She was adorned in a patriotic ensemble, complete with a miniature stars-and-stripes hat atop her head. The backdrop for the photos showcased Holiday Junction's iconic landmarks, creating a picturesque setting for the tourists' keepsake memories.

Radley's eyes widened with surprise, a mixture of disbelief and amusement dancing in his gaze. He turned to me, his voice tinged with laughter. "Violet, is that... a dog in a Fourth of July outfit? And she's the village mayor?"

I couldn't help but chuckle at his reaction. "Yes, Radley, that's Paisley, the beloved Boston terrier and honorary mayor of our quirky little village. She's quite the celebrity around here. Tourists love getting their photos taken with her as a fun holiday tradition."

As we watched the scene unfold, I noticed the joyful banter between the tourists and Paisley's entourage. Kristine Whitlock, her human caretaker, dressed in coordinating patriotic attire, ensured that each visitor had a memorable experience. The scene was a harmonious blend of laughter, wagging tails, and heartfelt smiles, all set against the backdrop of Holiday Junction's charm.

A mischievous glint sparkled in Radley's eyes as he leaned closer to me, and his voice filled with playful banter. "So, Violet, if Paisley is the mayor, does that mean she holds the key to all the village's secrets?"

I grinned, playing along with his jest. "Oh, absolutely. She knows where all the bones are buried, both literally and metaphorically. But don't worry, I promise not to let her spill the beans."

Our laughter mingled with the joyous atmosphere that surrounded us as we soaked in the whimsical scene. It was a testament to the unique spirit of Holiday Junction, a place where even a four-legged mayor could capture the hearts of visitors and locals alike.

As Paisley's photo session continued, Radley and I exchanged lighthearted banter and playful teasing, our words punctuated by laughter. We shared a moment of carefree merriment, a delightful interlude amidst the deeper mysteries that beckoned us.

"Why don't you get some candids and I'll ask if they mind if we take photos for the *Junction Journal*," I told him.

As the sound of the shutter clicked, capturing the joyous expressions of the tourists alongside Paisley, I knew that this moment would be etched in Radley's memories.

Behind us, the air was filled with the sounds of cheers and patriotic music as families lined the sidewalks, waving flags and eagerly anticipating the parade.

"Room 3 is open if you want to stand on the balcony and take some photos." Kristine had gotten an employee of the inn to come take her place so she could talk to me. "Is this a cousin?"

Kristine and I had gotten to be pretty good friends, and she knew I was an only child, which was probably why she assumed Radley was my cousin or some sort of relative.

"Kristine Whitlock, this is Radley Jordon, the newest citizen of Holiday Junction and journalist at the *Junction Journal*." My words left quite the impact on her.

"I, well, I," she stuttered. Kristine was in her sixties with salt-and-pepper hair. She had a few wrinkles on her forehead and long smile lines that stayed etched after she stopped smiling. "I'm shocked the Stricklands hired someone else."

"You and me both." I left out the details about macing the poor guy. "I'm so glad because he can go to Room 3 and take some photos while I go check on a new story."

"If Room 3 happens to be open, is there any way I can take that room since I'm booked already?" he asked.

"Yes, of course." Kristine had us follow her inside of the cute inn.

The inside was more of an open setting with a lounging area you had to walk through to get to the back wall, where a woman waited behind the counter.

"We have gadgets in the rooms for our guests' electronics. If you need to purchase anything, you can take a right out of the inn, and just a couple of blocks down next to Brewing Bean is the Jovial General Store." Kristine told this to all the guests. I'd heard her exposition so many times, I could do her job. "I'm guessing since you're a paperman, you have a lot of things to plug in."

"And you can head on up and start taking those photos before the parade starts." I heard the clock on the wall ding ten o'clock a.m., the start time of the parade.

Where had the morning already gone?

"Where are your bags?" Kristine asked.

"Good question. I need to check on that." He chuckled, not needing to say anything more. "The guy at the airport told me not to worry about it. He'd get them here once they arrived."

The Holiday Junction Airport was tiny. It had one runway with one building that was literally just an open building with Dave, a rooster, as a security guard. Or at least he was considered head of security.

Apparently, Dave could sniff out anything better than a security dog, and since he was locally owned by Diffy Delk, the attorney, Dave got the job.

"Rhett," Kristine and I said in unison before we broke out in laughter.

Radley sighed, shaking his head and stuffing his hands in his pockets as the camera bag dangled over his shoulder.

"I'm not sure if I'm going to get used to the place." He smiled and looked at me. His amusement was cute.

"Room 3." Kristine walked behind the counter and plucked the key off one of the rings hanging on the wall. They'd yet to go to the keyless or even card-style keys for the rooms. The inn was still a very nice place to stay. "If you need anything, just ask."

"I'm going to go get some photos. Make me worth my salt." He started up the steps and waved his card in the air.

"My oh my." Kristine hummed and tilted her head to the side as we watched Radley continue his journey up to Room 3. "Darren Strickland better watch out."

A laugh exploded out of me.

CHAPTER FIVE

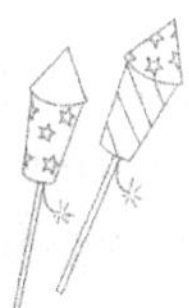

As the vibrant rays of the July sun illuminated the streets of Holiday Junction, I found myself standing in front of the Winston Art Gallery. The gallery, nestled between quaint storefronts, boasted an air of elegance and sophistication. Today, however, the place had undergone a patriotic transformation in honor of the Fourth of July.

The sound of the high school band and cheers of the participants along the parade route were easily heard. The village was small, and even though there were many streets, they weren't very far apart.

The gallery's windows showcased an impressive display of artwork that celebrated the spirit of the holiday. One striking painting showed the American flag billowing majestically, its stars and stripes capturing the essence of freedom and unity. Splashes of red, white, and blue adorned the surrounding canvases, showcasing various artistic interpretations of the nation's heritage.

Stepping inside, I marveled at the gallery's interior. Soft, ambient lighting cast a warm glow upon the walls, showcasing an impressive collection of art. The scent of freshly painted canvases mingled with the subtle fragrance of flowers, creating an atmosphere that was both inspiring and inviting.

I had no idea what a good piece of art even looked like, but I knew what I thought was pretty.

As I scanned the room, searching for someone to speak with, my eyes settled on a young woman emerging from the back.

She approached me with a friendly smile, but her eyes held a hint of unease. Her name tag pinned on her charcoal gray blazer was etched with her name, Emily.

"I'm sorry, but we're closed today due to some unforeseen circumstances," Emily said, her voice tinged with disappointment. She pointed at a small plaque on the door that was turned to indicate that the gallery was temporarily closed.

I nodded understandingly, my curiosity piqued by the mysterious turn of events. “I’m Violet Rhinehammer with the *Junction Journal*. I was hoping to speak with you about Graham Winston.”

“Oh. I see. The police made the announcement?” she asked.

“Announcement?” I asked.

She tugged in her lips. She was a young woman with a slender figure and an understated elegance in her appearance. Her dark, wavy hair framed her face, falling gracefully over her shoulders. Emily possessed an aura of quiet confidence, her every movement deliberate and poised.

Her attire mirrored the art gallery’s sophistication. Under her tailored charcoal gray blazer, she wore a crisp white blouse, which was paired with a knee-length black skirt. The ensemble exuded a sense of professionalism and attention to detail. A delicate silver pendant graced her neck, hinting at a touch of personal style.

My journalist instincts kicked into high gear, sensing that there was more to the story than met the eye.

Emily's warm smile conveyed genuine warmth and friendliness, creating an inviting atmosphere within the gallery. Her hazel eyes sparkled with a mix of professionalism and curiosity, reflecting her passion for the art world. She possessed a deep knowledge of the pieces within the gallery, and her love for art shone through in every interaction.

"We are closed for an employees-only memorial for Mr. Winston." Emily sucked in a deep breath.

"Is there anything you can share with me? I'm here to uncover the truth, Emily. Perhaps there's something I can do to help," I suggested.

Emily's eyes darted nervously, and her voice lowered until it was barely above a whisper. "I wish I could tell you more, Violet, but I've been instructed to keep it under wraps for now. Please understand that it's a sensitive matter, and I'm sure the police will give a statement you can publish."

I nodded, recognizing the gravity of the situation. "I understand, Emily. If there's anything you can share in the future, please don't hesitate to reach out. The truth has a way of revealing itself, and I'm here to shed light on any hidden secrets. After all, we want Graham's killer to be caught."

Emily's expression softened, as though she appreciated my understanding. "Thank you, Violet. I'll remember that. For now, I must tend to matters here. Feel free to come back another time when the gallery reopens, and we can discuss art and the mysteries that surround it."

"Here's my card." I took my card out of my purse and handed it to her. "Call me anytime. Day or night."

I couldn't help but wonder how she fit into the larger puzzle and what role she might play in uncovering the truth behind this unexpected turn of events. She was definitely hiding something. I just wasn't sure what it was.

Yet.

As I reached for the door handle to leave the art gallery, Emily gently laid a hand on my arm, stopping me in my tracks. I turned to face her, and what I saw in her eyes sent a shiver down my spine. Fear, raw and palpable, gripped her features, replacing her usual composed demeanor.

"Violet, please," Emily pleaded in a voice barely above a whisper. "I don't want to be next. You have to be careful."

My heart skipped a beat, the gravity of the situation sinking in. The unexpected turn from a simple investigation sent shock waves through me. I knew I had to tread carefully, to gather the truth without putting myself or others in harm's way.

Emily, her voice trembling with fear, handed me a small piece of paper. "These names... These are people you should look into. They might have answers about Graham's death. But please be discreet. I'm scared, Violet."

Once I took the list from her trembling hand, I folded it carefully and placed it in my pocket. I met her gaze, and determination laced my voice. "I will do everything I can, Emily. I'll dig deeper, uncover the truth, and find justice for Graham. But I need you to trust me and stay safe. If you remember anything else or have any doubts, reach out to me. We're in this together."

A flicker of relief crossed Emily's face, mingled with lingering fear. "Thank you, Violet. I... I believe in you. Please, be careful."

We shared a brief, understanding nod before Emily retreated into the gallery, seeking solace in the familiar surroundings.

As the door closed behind her, I took a moment to gather my thoughts. The weight of the investigation had intensified, and the list of names now burning a hole in my pocket became my road map to uncovering the truth behind Graham's untimely demise.

If anyone knew anything, I would say it was Emily. She had worked closely with him, or had she? I was pretty sure she didn't put her name on the list. Her name automatically went on mine.

Stepping out onto the sunlit streets of Holiday Junction, I couldn't shake the sense of urgency that gripped me.

The quiet whispers of a small village held secrets, secrets that threatened to unravel the fabric of the community. If they went to great lengths to conceal the Merry Maker's identity, I could only imagine what someone who killed someone else would do.

With each step, I carried the weight of responsibility on my shoulders, determined to navigate the treacherous path ahead, uncover the truth, and bring justice to those who sought to silence Graham forever.

As I turned the corner to head toward Holiday Park, I saw the first signs of the floats as they took the circle and veered right. They were going toward the end of the route, the business district called Central Square. There, the hospital, police, and Welcome Center were located.

I noticed Radley was on the corner, snapping photos and even crouching down as if taking photos of someone on the catwalk.

"What's up?" I asked when I got closer to him.

"I'm waiting for Ms. Holiday Junction. She's quite the beauty." He was smitten with her, like most men in the village.

"Oh, Fern." I shrugged and leaned around him to see what float was next. "She's not that great."

He laughed and took his eye away from the sites of the camera.

"I think I see her float coming now." He moved the camera back to his face and continued to snap.

"Be sure you get Mayor Paisley," I told him before I excused myself to go back to the office where I would go over the list of people Emily had given me.

"Don't worry. I'll get them all," he said, the camera muffling his voice.

When Fern rode past on the back of Rhett Strickland's car, I couldn't help but notice how she took a little extra time to wave at our handsome, newest citizen before a big smile exposed her pearly whites.

Rhett Strickland—well, he was another story. He gunned the gas, causing the convertible to lurch forward.

Time seemed to slow as Fern, caught off guard by the sudden burst of speed, teetered backward in the seat. Her arms flailed in the air, and her legs kicked wildly as if she were doing an impromptu acrobatic routine. The sight was comical, making me bite my lip to suppress a fit of laughter.

"Oh, Fern!" I exclaimed, my voice filled with amusement. "Hold on tight!"

Fern's eyes widened in surprise, her laughter blending with shock and exhilaration. She tried to regain her balance, her hands gripping onto anything within reach, but her efforts were in vain.

With a final flail of her legs, she tumbled backward, disappearing as the convertible sped away.

I couldn't contain my laughter any longer. I doubled over on the sidewalk, tears streaming down my cheeks. It was a classic Rhett Strickland move. He was always finding ways to inject humor and spontaneity into the lives of Holiday Junction's residents.

As the echoes of my laughter subsided, I couldn't help but appreciate the joy that Fern brought to the town. Despite the unexpected turn of events, I knew that Fern would take it in stride, finding humor and delight even in the most unexpected circumstances.

With a smile lingering on my face, I dusted off my clothes and continued on my way toward the office, the memory of Fern's acrobatics etched into my mind.

It was just another reminder that in this charming town, laughter and camaraderie were woven into the fabric of everyday life, bringing a sense of lightheartedness to even the most ordinary moments. No killer on the loose was going to stop the feeling I'd found in my new home.

CHAPTER SIX

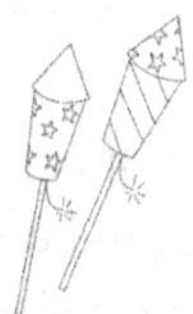

"Fern Banks," Radley said, sounding interested. "What's her deal? Was that guy her boyfriend? He seemed awfully annoyed with my taking her photo."

"Fern is available, if that's what you're asking. As for the guy"—I pulled the piece of paper that Emily had given me out of my pocket—"that's Rhett Strickland."

"As in Marge's nephew, right?" he asked, somehow knowing this piece of information.

"How do you know that?" I asked, handing him the piece of paper as we made our way through the crowd alongside the lake.

He stopped, so I did too. Then he looked at the piece of paper.

"What's this?" he asked, handing it back to me. He picked up the camera to start taking more candid snapshots of the people paddling around on large swan paddle boats, which had red, white, and blue sashes around their necks.

The Holiday Committee, of which Mama was a member, didn't leave anything untouched in the Fourth of July celebration. If an object had even an inch of open space, it got some sort of red, white, or blue thing on it.

The environment looked like a large firework had exploded, throwing up all the glitter over the entire village.

"While you were covering the parade, I went to Winston Art Gallery and met Emily, Graham's assistant." I shook the piece of paper. "When I asked her about Graham and told her I wanted to help, she was pretty apprehensive. There were employees in there, and they were gathered in mourning for him, but when I went to leave, she stopped me at the door."

"And she handed you this list of names." He snorted from behind the camera as he took a few more candid shots. This time, he was aiming the lens toward a group of children playing in the water fountain. They were letting their twirly whirls move by the falling water, not by the light summer breeze.

"That didn't sound so convincing." I pointed out that his tone reflected a little hint of apprehension.

"I think if someone would know the man, it would be his assistant," he said, not making a lick of sense to me. He sighed when he saw the look on my face. "For instance, she gave you a list. That means she's already been thinking about it. What if she's been thinking about it in a way that would make her not be on any sort of suspect list?"

"What would her motive be?" I asked, now following his line of thinking.

We started to walk again. This time, I pointed him toward the path between Holiday Park and the seaside, a faster way to the office by foot.

"So many things." Radley stopped at the shaved ice stand. "I'll take two American Snow Cones," he said and pulled out a five-dollar bill in exchange, telling the vendor to keep the change.

"Financial gain. Emily may have wanted to inherit or take control of the art gallery and believed that killing Graham was the only way to make it happen," he suggested and then handed me the snow cone.

"Thank you." I received the kind gesture. "Revenge," I added.

He nodded and used the spoon the vendor had stuck down in the compact icy treat to scoop up a bite.

"Emily may have had a personal grudge against Graham for some reason, such as mistreatment or abuse in the workplace, and sought revenge by killing him." I was throwing darts in the air to see what stuck.

"Jealousy. Emily may have been jealous of Graham's success and felt that killing him was the only way to level the playing field. I mean, art does seem like a dog-eat-dog field." Radley continued to munch on the snow cone, and I took the time while he was talking to eat some too.

"Blackmail. Emily may have had compromising information on Graham or vice versa and believed that killing him was the only way to keep it from getting out," I added. "Like, what if he had some bad dealings?"

"Maybe Graham was planning to retire and leave the gallery to someone Emily didn't like." He stuck his spoon up in the air as if he were having an ah-ha moment. "Emily saw this as a betrayal because she thought she should get the gallery? Loyalty."

"What if Emily was secretly in love with Graham and became jealous when he started dating someone else? Her jealousy turned into obsession, leading her to commit the crime." I started to laugh at how our crazy ideas had now become great theories.

"Graham and Emily had a falling out over a controversial art piece that he wanted to display in the gallery. Emily disagreed with the decision, and the argument turned violent." Radley hit on something.

"You know what?" I stopped.

"What?" he asked.

"When I was at Brewing Beans, Hazelynn told me that Graham had a lot of his gallery pieces in the coffee shop at one time. Then Victor Monroe accused Graham of forging a piece. What if instead of Emily, Victor and Graham's falling out over the controversial art piece ended up in an argument turned violent?"

"Where are you going?" Radley asked when I darted off in the opposite direction than we had been going.

"You go straight down that path, and it'll take you to the beach." I jutted my finger in the direction. "At the end, hang a left, and you'll go straight to the office. You can't miss it."

"You didn't answer my question." He threw his hand up in the air.

"I'm going to go see Hazelynn about that argument. I'll meet you at the office. You go start looking into these names." I took the piece of paper Emily gave me out of my pocket and handed it to him again. "I don't think Victor is on there."

"So..." He shook his head.

"If Emily was the assistant she's supposed to be, Victor Monroe would've been on that list. That makes me think she and Victor might have something to do with Graham's death." I smiled. My journalist gut feeling was telling me this had to be a lead to follow.

Radley didn't bat an eye when I told him I'd meet him. He did what I asked him to do, which was good. The newest *Junction Journal* employee and I didn't seem to have any tension between us.

With the Fourth of July festivities in full swing, I hurried through the streets, heading for Brewing Beans. The sun beamed down, warming my skin as I weaved through the crowded sidewalks. I had time to go through the list of names Emily had handed me, but something seemed off.

Victor was conspicuously missing. I couldn't help but wonder if he and Emily were in on something together. Emily's failure to mention their disagreement made her look all the more suspicious.

The downtown area was teeming with life, boutique shops and street vendors alike showcasing their patriotic window displays and merchandise.

The aromas of food trucks wafted through the air, blending with the scents of sizzling hot dogs, buttery popcorn, and the all-American apple pie. The cheerful chatter of families and friends created a lively atmosphere, and I found myself exchanging greetings with familiar faces as I continued on my mission.

As I zigzagged among the throngs of people, I admired the town's dedication to the holiday. Red, white, and blue bunting adorned storefronts, and American flags waved proudly from every street corner. My surroundings made a picturesque scene of small-town charm and unity.

Once I reached Brewing Beans, I quickly scanned the café, searching for Hazelynn.

"Hazelynn." I said her name when her back was to me as she stood behind the counter.

"Back again?" She smiled.

"I wanted to see if I could ask you a few questions about Graham." I tilted my head to the side, where we would have some private space for us to talk.

"You have some leads?" she asked, her eyes big and round.

"I'm trying to tie a connection." I hesitated to tell her about the list of names, but I was doing my journalistic job. "I went to see Emily at the Winston Art Gallery. She gave me a list of names, and there was a name not on there. Victor Monroe."

"That's odd," Hazelynn said immediately. "Because she was with Graham the day he and Victor were in here arguing. Then she mentioned something to me about how Victor came in there all the time, causing trouble for Graham."

"You'd think Victor would be the first one on her list of people for me to look into," I said.

None of this made any sort of sense, unless Emily had an ulterior motive for not placing Victor on the list. It was time to confront Emily about the omission of Victor's name.

"Hazelynn," Hershal called, gesturing to the bustling coffee shop for her to help.

"I've got to go, but if I remember anything else, I'll call you." Hazelynn turned to Hershal. "Coming!"

I stepped back outside and took my phone out to call Radley but realized I didn't have his number. I wanted him to do a quick search on Victor Monroe but then decided to just do one on my phone.

Cell service was spotty in the village, but I was able to pull up a photo of the man.

Victor Monroe was middle-aged with a stocky build and a slightly balding head. He had a thick, bushy mustache and a square jawline. His eyes appeared to be dark and piercing.

In the photo, he was dressed in an expensive suit and wore a gold watch on his wrist. That was one thing I did know. Fashion. Victor Monroe was fashionable. More than Graham, and I thought he was all to-do in his fancy suits.

My eyes darted around the crowd as I tried to decide which way to head back to the office, where I could do some digging around on Victor or see if Radley had gotten anywhere. Then I spotted Emily, just down the street, engaged in a deep conversation with a man who looked a lot like the photo on my phone.

My heart raced as I contemplated my next move. Was Emily involved in Graham's murder? Or was she simply caught in the crossfire of a bitter rivalry?

One thing was certain. I needed to get to the bottom of this story.

I took a deep breath, straightened my shoulders, and proceeded toward Emily and Victor. It was time to confront the truth, whatever it might be.

"Violet." The way Emily said my name indicated that she was surprised. "I, um," she stuttered, shifting her eyes between Victor and me.

My finger jabbed at the buttons on my phone screen to bring up the memo app. I hit Record.

"Victor Monroe?" I stuck my hand out. "Violet Rhinehammer from the *Junction Journal*. I'm doing a story on Graham Winston's murder. Tell me about the public argument you and the victim had about the forgery you accused him of."

I stuck my phone in his face.

"I'm sorry. I'm not doing any interviews." He pushed my hand away.

"I'm taking your response as a reason of omission," I said into the phone, which I then turned on Emily. "I'm assuming since you left Victor off the list of potential people who would've killed your boss, you and Victor have some sort of side deal going."

Emily stuttered and sputtered. Victor twisted his chin and furrowed his brows at her.

"Why else would you be meeting in the crowded streets where no one could really see you when you told me you were closed for an all-day memorial just for employees of the Winston Art Gallery?" I shoved the phone in her face. "Or are you two trying to come up with a plan for when Chief Strickland calls you in his office after I publish these photos in the paper with little tidbits about why the police should look at you as potential suspects?"

"What photos?" Victor appeared shocked but not as shocked as when I turned the phone around and snapped a few quick pictures of him and Emily standing together.

"These." I smiled and twisted around to walk off. This was the kind of journalism that really got my blood pumping.

"Violet! Violet!" Emily called after me, but I ignored her.

It wasn't until she came running up behind me and put her hand on my arm that I flipped around.

"Fine." Emily shook her head. There was a flat line across her lips. "We will meet you at the seaside bar tonight at nine."

"Why nine? Why not now?" I asked. "So you'll have time to think about what story you want to tell me? Or think up a good alibi for the police?"

"So we can tell you what's really been going on in the art world," Victor interrupted, catching my attention. "Before anyone else gets murdered."

This story was much bigger than I'd initially thought and went well beyond Graham Winston's death.

CHAPTER SEVEN

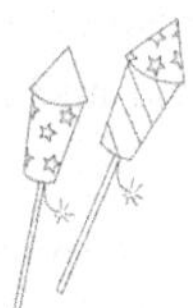

The trolley was pulling into the trolley stop going away from Holiday Park. Hitching a ride to the seaside that way would be faster than maneuvering around the crowded downtown area to take the path.

"Did you get some good shots of the parade?" Goldie asked when I sat down in the seat behind her.

"I'm not sure. I let Radley take them." I had more important things to do, I thought. Like trying to get some information out of Emily.

I scooted up on the edge of the seat and leaned a little closer to Goldie so no one else would hear.

"I know the police haven't given a report on Graham Winston's murder." The trolley lurched, causing me to grab the handrail attached to my seat. "I went to see Emily, his assistant, and I was wondering if you knew them that well? Or could tell me anything you might've seen."

As a journalist, it was my job to get to the nitty-gritty details. From what I'd found in cases such as Graham's, the tiny details were where the biggest clues were hidden. Goldie Bennett knew a lot of people, saw a lot of things, and heard a lot of stuff.

"Are we on the record or off?" she asked, obviously armed with something.

"Who are you?" I teased, reminding her I'd always kept her name and the information she'd given me out of the newspaper and off my lips when relying pertinent information to authorities.

"As the trolley driver in Holiday Junction, I have a unique opportunity to overhear countless conversations and observe the townspeople's comings and goings. When it came to Graham's death, I inadvertently became privy to several crucial details that could potentially shed light on things leading up to people who might've wanted to..." She clicked her tongue, implying murder.

"Like what kind of things?" I asked, actually happy to have taken the trolley, though it was proving to be slower, not faster. Goldie had to drive slowly due to the pedestrians as well as the extra stops put along the way so festivalgoers could take the trolley at any given moment.

"One day, as I drove my usual route, I overheard a heated argument between Graham and Cassandra Firbank, the local art teacher who had dated Graham for a long time before their recent breakup." Goldie mentioned one of the names on Emily's list.

"They dated, and now they're broken up?" I asked. This was all news to me, and I wanted to make sure I'd heard her correctly. Much laughter and chatter came from the other passengers, so making sure I'd gotten the correct information was crucial.

"They did." She nodded, keeping her eyes on the road. "Their voices carried through the open window of the trolley, and although I couldn't make out every word, I could sense the tension in the air. You know those schoolkids at the end of the day can get really rowdy."

She had lost me a little.

"Schoolkids?" I asked.

"Yes. If the other trolley driver who has the school route is out, sometimes I fill in. On this particular day, it was the last week of school." She had given me a timeframe.

"Were they broken up then?" I asked.

"The argument seemed to center around a secret that Graham had discovered, which had ultimately led to their breakup. So they weren't broken up when I heard the argument." She stopped the trolley and let a few people off and a few others on before she continued her story. "Now that school is out for the summer, the teachers still have to go in. Cassandra had missed the trolley going to the school about a week ago, and I wasn't busy, so I told her to jump in. I noticed she appeared increasingly distraught and anxious. I've known her for a long time, and as a creative, she says she often seems lost in her thoughts, and her usual warm demeanor was replaced with a cold, distant attitude. When I noticed that, I wondered if Cassandra's behavior was somehow connected to the information Graham had uncovered and the subsequent argument I had overheard."

"You are very observant," I told her and continued to type her thoughts and information in the Notes app on my phone. "Did she tell you what she found out about Graham?"

"No," she said with a frown. "I also recalled a conversation I had overheard between two of Graham's close friends after I picked them up from a liquid lunch at the bar."

"The Jiggle Joint?" I asked, making Goldie snicker.

"Yep," she confirmed and brought the trolley to an abrupt stop. She turned around and got the attention of a family with a teenage son. "Please keep your arms in the trolley," she told him. "We can't be going to the emergency room when they get sliced off by hitting something. Read the sign."

She turned back in her seat and pointed at the sign of rules for trolley passengers above her head.

"Back to my story." She hit the gas. "They mentioned that Graham had been acting strangely, hinting that he had stumbled upon some dangerous information that could put his life at risk. The friends speculated that the information might have been related to his breakup with Cassandra."

"That means they had to have broken up within the last few weeks." I really wanted to know what Cassandra knew and why Emily would have her on the list.

"Do you know the names of his friends?" I asked.

"Patrick O'Connor," she said, referring to another person on Emily's list. "Patrick designed Graham's art gallery. He and Graham had been friends since their college days. And Vern McKenna."

"Vern?" I didn't see his name on the list, but I knew him very well.

"Mm-hmm." She brought the trolley to a stop right in front of the office. "As a respected member of the Holiday Junction community and a grandmother to my little babies, you know I don't want to get entangled in a potentially dangerous situation. I have my own family to think about."

"Mum's the word." I stood up and used my finger like a zipper across my lips. "If you hear anything else, please let me know. Between me and you, I think there's more to Graham's murder than meets the eye."

I heard the squeak of Goldie pulling the trolley's lever before the accordion doors slammed shut. I made my way up to the office.

The sound of laughter filtered through the open windows, and for a moment, I wondered if it was just an echo of the people down at the beach enjoying the Fourth of July festival. When I turned to look, I noticed where the police tape had been taken down and the carnival rides had resumed.

"Violet," Darren called out with a hint of laughter. "I can't believe you didn't tell me about Radley being here."

I walked into my office, where the two men were sitting in the chairs, all reclined and chatting like two old friends.

"I haven't had a chance to talk to you with the parade and all the activities." I smiled and walked over to him after he stood up to hug me.

"I can't believe you failed to mention you were dating Darren Strickland." Radley looked shocked. "Nor can I believe you scored a woman as smart and ambitious as Violet."

"I love that you maced him last night." Darren clapped his hands. "Classic."

"How do you two know each other?" I asked and noticed Radley had already written something on the whiteboard as well as the names Emily had given me.

"Aunt Marge had taken me to a newspaper conference. We met there." Darren failed to mention that Radley's dad and Aunt Marge had once dated, so I didn't say anything. "We had the best time running around."

"Yeah. Can you imagine two teenage boys running around in Vegas without any adult supervision?" Radley asked.

"I don't think I want to imagine that." I laughed.

"I was telling Radley he should come down to the bar. Grab some lunch off the taco truck," Darren said. "He said he had to work on the murder."

"Your mama drives a hard bargain," I said. "But go on. I've got this. I need to do a little research, and the quiet office will do some good."

"Are you sure? It's my first day," Radley noted.

"Of course I'm sure. It's a holiday week. Go. Have fun." I encouraged him. "Darren, take him. I'll be at the bar tonight."

"You will?" Darren asked me.

"Yes, and so will you." I pointed at Radley. "We are going to meet Emily and Victor Monroe there at nine p.m."

I walked over to the whiteboard.

"How did that happen?" Radley asked.

"Remember when I told you to go back to the office and take the list?" I didn't really mean for him to answer me as I continued to tell what had happened as I got the information from Hazelynn. "When I left the coffee shop, I noticed Emily was talking with the man I'd googled. I knew it was Victor."

"Do you think she and Victor knocked Graham off?" Radley asked.

Darren shook his head.

"What?" Radley's brows pinched.

"You two have some sort of language between you. I don't get the drive you seem to have on this murder." Darren laughed. "Come on. Let's go or Violet will keep you here talking about this endlessly and you'll never make it down to the bar."

"Go. I'll chase some of these leads and catch up with you tonight," I told Radley. "And I hope we can meet up after my little visit with Emily and Victor."

"You owe me a Ferris wheel ride," Darren said, reminding me about his request that I go to the carnival with him while it was in town for the Fourth of July festival.

Darren was a kid at heart, which was why we put the Merry Maker sign on the beach near the carnival.

With the office quiet, I wanted to transcribe all my notes from Goldie and everything Hazelynn had said onto the whiteboard and see where things connected to one another.

I stood in front of the whiteboard, which had become a murder investigation board. With my arms crossed, I scanned the list of suspects.

First was Emily. I wasn't so sure what her possible motive could've been, but I did know Radley and I had come up with a lot of speculative theories. When I saw her with Victor, another suspect who had a solid motive for committing the murder, it made me wonder if Victor and Emily were in on something that led to Graham's murder.

Had Graham found out Emily had given some information to Victor, his number one enemy? Or did Graham know something about Victor and Emily that would cause them to get rid of him? If they did have some big secret, it was buried with Graham.

Or so they might think. In my experience, most buried things had a way of resurfacing. And secrets involving murder never stayed hidden for long.

Then there was Victor. Even before I saw him with Emily, he was already the primary suspect on my list.

The mere fact that he and Graham had an argument in which he accused Graham of forgery mattered. From what I'd googled, forgery was the most immoral, if not illegal, thing an art dealer could do. If Victor accused Graham of forgery, why would Victor have killed Graham? Wouldn't it have been the other way around?

From what I'd gathered, there was more to their relationship than just this whole forgery theory.

I would definitely ask him about that tonight when I met up with him and Emily.

What about Cassandra? I couldn't forget what Goldie had overheard. What secret did Graham uncover that would make him and Cassandra break up?

I couldn't wait to find out what Patrick O'Connor and Vern had to say. According to Goldie, they'd discussed the possibility that Graham's life could've been in danger.

That made me think Patrick and Vern were probably the two most important people to see. If they had some information that involved Emily, Cassandra, or Victor, then that would be my first big lead.

"What are you doing here?" Mama asked, scaring the living daylights out of me. "Didn't you hear me call your name when I came in the door?"

"No. I was so wrapped up in my thoughts about this investigation and how to go about writing an article for the paper on it that I tuned out the world." I sighed. "How has the festival been today? Did you get to the parade?"

"One question at time. Dear me." Mama sounded exhausted. "I've been running all over, handing out my brochures and making sure everyone comes to the Leisure Center for the big opening tomorrow night for Fireworks Bingo."

"Fireworks Bingo?" I snorted. "That sounds dangerous."

"Only if you consider free food, free entertainment, and great prizes dangerous." Mama walked over and looked at the board. "Is that Cassandra Firbank, the art teacher?"

"Yeah." I leaned back and looked at Mama. "Do you know her?"

"Know her?" Mama put her hand on her hip. "Don't you listen to anything I tell you? She's going to be teaching art classes at the Leisure Center full-time during the rest of the summer and part-time when school starts back up."

"You didn't tell me about any sort of art classes," I said.

"It's right here." Mama turned and grabbed one of the Leisure Center brochures off my desk. She unfolded the trifold and pointed at the bullet points listed under the activities. "I told you, and I recall you laughing, saying it was a paint-by-numbers class."

"Oh. I did say that." I couldn't believe I'd forgotten that quick conversation we'd had about all the activities she'd planned.

"I recall you telling me that was childish, and I told you painting and art is a big thing to help keep our minds active. And to think you pooh-poohed it." Mama tsked. "One of these days, Violet Rhinehammer, you're gonna realize your mama isn't a dummy."

"Mama, I never called you a dummy. I'm sorry. You were right," I apologized and put my arm around her shoulder.

It was best to apologize and go on instead of trying to plead my case when she was right about doing whatever we could to stay active as we aged.

"Your Leisure Center is going to be a good thing," I said. "And I'd like to meet Cassandra."

"She dated Graham?" Mama read the board. "She told me she wasn't in a relationship anymore and had a lot of free time to work the rest of the summer after our big opening."

"That's because she and Graham broke up over some big secret Graham had found out." I looked at Mama.

"I know that look." She shook her finger at me. "You want me to meddle in her business."

"I'm not saying meddle. Maybe just see if she's okay. I mean, her boyfriend is dead." I shrugged. "And possibly get an alibi."

"Alibi?" Mama jerked up, her voice shrill. "Why on earth do you think she would've killed him?"

"Someone told me they'd overheard Graham and Cassandra arguing. Cassandra didn't want Graham to tell his big secret, and I don't know why. If she didn't want it to come out, it had to be something that would affect people, and a secret that big just might get someone killed if they were willing to tell it."

"I'm not going to do no such thing. You can do it," Mama said, putting the task on me. "I need an art teacher, and if I go around asking about her ex-boyfriend and if she killed him, she might quit, and I can't have that right now. Besides, you have no real hard evidence she would do such a thing. And she's nice."

"Fine. I'll ask her myself." I could tell by Mama's stance that she wouldn't budge. If I wanted answers, I was going to have to get them myself. "Is she going to be at Fireworks Bingo tomorrow?"

"All the volunteers are going to be helping out, and that means Cassandra too." Mama was all bent out of shape about my wanting to ask Cassandra. "If you make a scene, I'll be mad. I've made a lot of friends around here, and you aren't going to use this job to hurt that."

"Mama, what are you saying?" I asked.

"I'm saying that when we lived in Normal, you did whatever you needed to do to get that next big story, not worry about the wake you left behind. I lost a lot of friends because you went around sticking that camera in people's faces trying to get the next big scoop." Mama yammered on and on, naming names and telling me situations I had no idea about.

"What was I supposed to do?" I asked, somewhat disturbed to think I'd caused Mama to lose friends. "Not use my education to do my job and only report on births and potlucks in the church's undercroft?"

Mama furrowed her brows and sucked in her lips.

"My goodness, Mama, I've got a job to do, and I can't help whose toes I step on. Maybe their toes won't be so sensitive unless they have something to hide." I grabbed my bag off the desk and swung it over my shoulder. "I've got people to see about a murder. Make sure you watch your back because the company you're keeping these days just might have their own days numbered."

CHAPTER EIGHT

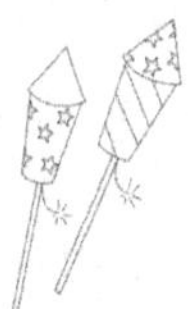

While I was talking to Mama, it occurred to me that I should also visit Victor's art gallery. If he and Graham were these big rivals, then someone who worked for Victor had to know. It was what they might tell me that piqued my interest.

I had no idea what I would find out from Emily, and I walked away with a list of potential suspects. Although I didn't know where to find Cassandra, I knew she was going to be at Mama's Leisure Center tomorrow night, which gave me some time to check out the others on the list.

When I saw Emily with Victor, I couldn't help but question why he wasn't on her list. It only made sense to me to go to his art gallery and see what information I could gather.

Doing that would only benefit me for my meeting with him and Emily tonight.

Prepared. Being prepared with a lot of information before a meeting was a hallmark of a good journalist.

As I hopped onto the trolley, my excitement grew with each passing moment. Today was the day I'd venture into the mountains of Holiday Junction, an area I had yet to explore. Known for its art district, where

Victor's art gallery was located, this part of town held a promise of hidden gems and artistic wonders.

Goldie Bennett, the lively trolley driver, greeted me with her usual spirited charm.

"Art district." She snorted, staring at me over the top of her nose with a curious eye. "I didn't figure you for one of them, but to each their own." She shrugged and slammed the doors closed.

As the trolley meandered toward the mountains, Goldie began regaling me with tales of the art district's rich history. She shared stories of renowned artists who had once called this place home, their vibrant creativity breathing life into the very fabric of the community.

Riding through the picturesque streets of the art district, I couldn't help but be captivated by the beauty that unfolded before my eyes. It was like stepping into a living canvas. Every detail was carefully curated to create a harmonious blend of charm and creativity.

Colorful storefronts lined the streets, each one boasting its unique character and artistic flair. Delicate floral arrangements spilled out onto the sidewalks from flower shops, infusing the air with a fragrant symphony of scents. The facades of boutique shops were adorned with vibrant window displays, showcasing handcrafted treasures that beckoned passersby to explore further.

The buildings exuded a timeless elegance, their architectural styles ranging from Victorian-inspired designs with ornate balconies and intricate ironwork to modern facades with clean lines and large windows that bathed the interiors in natural light. Ivy climbed gracefully up the sides of some structures, adding a touch of whimsy to the scene.

As the trolley passed, I caught glimpses of pedestrians taking leisurely strolls along the sidewalk. Artists holding paintbrushes and sketchbooks found inspiration in the surrounding beauty, while locals and tourists meandered from one shop to another, their faces illuminated with curiosity and excitement.

The sound of laughter and animated conversations filled the air, creating a palpable vibrant energy. The art district was clearly not just a place to shop or admire art—it was a gathering spot for kindred spirits, a community united by a shared love for creativity.

The sunlight filtered through the canopy of trees that lined the streets, casting dappled shadows on the pavement. Colorful clusters of flowers bloomed in window boxes and hanging baskets, their petals dancing in the gentle breeze. This scene seemed to exist outside of time. The present melded seamlessly with the past, and the pursuit of artistic expression was celebrated.

As the trolley continued its leisurely journey, I couldn't help but feel a sense of gratitude for being able to witness the art district's beauty firsthand. In this haven of creativity, where the picturesque streets whispered stories of inspiration, I knew that I was fortunate to be a part of such a vibrant and enchanting community.

For a moment, I caught myself picturing what it would look like to live in this part of Holiday Junction.

"The art district traces its origins back to the early settlers who sought refuge in the mountains, finding solace and inspiration amidst the serene beauty of the landscape," Goldie told me. "Over the years, artists from various backgrounds and disciplines gravitated toward the area, drawn in by the tranquil surroundings and the opportunity to immerse themselves in their craft."

It truly was like I was in an entirely different town—a different country, for that matter.

"As you can see, there's not a speck of Fourth of July celebration up here. The art district became a haven for painters, sculptors, photographers, and artisans of all kinds, forming a vibrant community centered around the celebration of creativity," she said and pointed at a sign describing the history of this area as the trolley passed by.

"Long before it was officially called the Art District, artists gathered in makeshift studios and opened their doors to curious visitors, showcasing their works and engaging in lively discussions about their artistic visions. This collaborative spirit laid the foundation for the close-knit community that the art district is known for today." She laughed. "We down the mountain called them hippies. But as the reputation of the art district grew, it attracted art enthusiasts, collectors, and tourists from near and far, eager to experience the magic that emanated from this creative hub. The local government recognized the district's cultural significance and invested in its development, supporting the establishment of galleries, boutiques, and art-related businesses."

She abruptly stopped the trolley and turned around in her seat to talk to me.

"That's when Victor Monroe opened his art gallery right there." She pointed. "Gallery 360."

The building looked like an architectural ingenuity with its unique design and distinctive features. The exterior of the gallery was adorned with large glass panels that served as windows, letting natural light flood the interior and allowing me to see inside and get a glimpse of the artistic treasures inside.

With a final burst of enthusiasm, Goldie bid me farewell, urging me to explore and embrace the magic that the mountains had to offer.

"Take your time. Before you come back to town, you should try Palette Café. It's good, and you might find Cassandra in there." Goldie was smart enough to know that I wasn't taking time out of the busy Fourth of July schedule to tour the art district.

She'd already known that I'd been investigating Graham's death, and since she mentioned the café, she knew I needed to talk to Cassandra, though she didn't tell me directly because like she'd said earlier, she wanted to stay anonymous.

I could provide her with anonymity.

Stepping off the trolley, I took in the crisp mountain air, ready to immerse myself in the art district's vibrant energy and uncover the truth that lay within its creative embrace.

There was no time to dilly-dally, so I made Gallery 360 my first stop.

The building itself was a blend of contemporary elements and artistic touches. It featured clean lines and sleek surfaces, lending a modern and sophisticated vibe to the structure. Vibrant murals adorned the walls, showcasing the talent of local artists and serving as an enticing invitation to step inside and explore the world of art.

As visitors entered Gallery 360, they were greeted by an open and spacious layout, allowing the artwork to take center stage.

The white walls created a gallery-like ambiance and provided a blank canvas for the art to make its statement. Adjustable track lighting illuminated each piece with precision, casting a spotlight on its intricate details and vibrant colors.

These were just a few things I'd noticed right off the bat that were vastly different from Graham's gallery. That made me wonder why Graham's gallery wasn't located in this district.

"Can I help you?" The employee who had greeted everyone must've noticed that I'd tried to slip past them.

"I'm looking for Victor Monroe." I noticed the name on the employee's tag read Benjamin Clark.

"I'm sorry. Mr. Monroe isn't here. Did you have an appointment?" He eyeballed my camera bag.

"I'm Violet Rhinehammer with the *Junction Journal*. I'm meeting Mr. Monroe tonight at the bar along the seaside. But I noticed your name tag. You knew Graham Winston." I watched as his jaw tensed. "And by your reaction, it wasn't a good acquaintance."

"I didn't give a reaction," he said, unaware of how his body language had changed.

"Since Victor isn't here and I'm meeting him later anyways, can I ask you a few questions?" I asked.

"You want to take the VIP gallery tour?" he asked when another person with a name tag on walked by.

"I guess." I hesitated and looked at him, wondering what he was up to.

"It'll be two hundred dollars cash." He held out his hand.

I laughed out loud, but he didn't seem to think it was very funny.

"Are you saying I have to pay for information?" I asked.

"The VIP tour comes with questions and answers if you pay cash." He shrugged and turned to walk away. "Come back when you'd like to take that special tour of the history of the galleries located here and in the town of Holiday Junction."

"Ah," I sighed and got it. If I wanted any information concerning the history of the two gallery owners, Graham and Victor, I was going to have to pay Benjamin for it. "Fine. I'd love the VIP tour right now."

I dug down into my bag.

"I'll take payment during the tour." He shifted his eyes and gestured for me to stop trying to pull out my wallet, as if someone was going to see me pay him off. "Right this way."

As I followed Benjamin Clarke through the halls of Gallery 360, I couldn't help but be captivated by his presence. Tall and slender, he exuded an air of quiet confidence as he moved with grace and purpose. His wavy chestnut hair fell effortlessly across his forehead, framing his chiseled features and piercing blue eyes that seemed to hold a depth of artistic insight.

Dressed in tailored trousers and a crisp white shirt with rolled-up sleeves, Benjamin emanated a sense of refined elegance. His attire complemented his artistic persona, a perfect blend of sophistication and creativity. I noticed a smudge of paint on his hand, a subtle reminder of his dedication to his craft.

As we walked through the gallery, Benjamin's passion for art shone through in his every word. He spoke with an animated enthusiasm, gesturing toward the paintings and sculptures that adorned the walls. His eyes sparkled with an infectious energy as he shared the stories behind each work of art, revealing the inspiration, techniques, and emotions that shaped its creation.

With every step, Benjamin's gestures became more animated, his hands moving gracefully through the air, bringing the art to life through his descriptions. He possessed an innate ability to bridge the gap between the artwork and the viewer, effortlessly guiding me through each piece's visual journey.

His voice carried a gentle cadence, rich with an artistic appreciation for the subtleties and nuances of every brushstroke, every lump of clay. As we lingered near a striking abstract painting, he explained its symbolism and the emotions it evoked, allowing me to see beyond the surface and truly connect with the artist's intent.

In the warm glow of the gallery's track lighting, Benjamin seemed to radiate a creative energy that was both inspiring and contagious. His passion for art was infectious, and I found myself completely immersed in his world as he revealed the stories woven within each masterpiece.

As Benjamin continued the tour, his genuine enthusiasm and love for art ignited a newfound appreciation within me. I realized that art was not just about aesthetics but about evoking emotions, sparking conversations, and transcending boundaries. Through Benjamin's guidance, Gallery 360 came alive, transforming from a mere collection of artworks into a tapestry of human expression.

He was not only an artist but a true storyteller, using his creative genius to captivate and inspire all who crossed his path, making me wonder why he was on Emily's list of suspects and how he and Graham had intersected.

I couldn't let the opportunity slip away. As Benjamin led me through the vibrant halls of Gallery 360, I decided it was time to address the elephant in the room and why I was paying him two hundred dollars. With a deep breath, I mustered the courage to interrupt our tour.

"Benjamin," I began, my voice tinged with curiosity, "I have to ask you something. Why were you on Emily's list of suspects for Graham's murder? And how did you know him?"

Benjamin's eyes widened slightly. A flicker of surprise crossed his face before he composed himself. He paused for a moment, contemplating his response, and then turned toward me, his gaze steady and open.

"Violet, I understand your need for answers. I assure you, my connection to Graham was purely professional," he replied, his voice calm and measured. "We collaborated on several art exhibitions in the past, exploring different themes and artistic styles. However, our relationship was strictly artistic, and I deeply respected him as a mentor and a colleague."

I listened intently, eager to discover the truth behind Emily's suspicions. Pressing further, I asked, "But why would Emily include you on her list? Did she have a specific reason to suspect you?"

Benjamin's brow furrowed, and he paused to gather his thoughts. "I can only speculate, Violet. Perhaps Emily's perception was clouded by certain misunderstandings or personal bias. It is unfortunate, but sometimes even the closest of colleagues can harbor hidden resentments or conflicting motivations."

My mind raced, trying to piece together the puzzle. Emily's list seemed to be a key to the truth, but the motives behind her suspicions remained elusive. I couldn't help but pose the question that weighed heavily on my mind.

"Benjamin, I have to ask, did you have any involvement in Graham's death?" I asked, my voice steady but tinged with urgency.

Sadness flickered in Benjamin's eyes, and he shook his head slowly. "No, Violet, I had no reason or desire to harm Graham. We may have had our artistic differences at times, but we shared a deep appreciation for art and a mutual respect. I would never resort to such a drastic measure."

His words sounded sincere, but I needed more than just his reassurances. I asked, "Can anyone vouch for your whereabouts on the night of the murder? An alibi that can support your innocence?"

A faint smile played on Benjamin's lips as he replied, "Yes, indeed. I was at a local artist gathering that evening, surrounded by fellow creatives who can confirm my presence. They saw firsthand that I was immersed in discussions about art, far removed from any dark intentions. I'm more than happy to give names to Chief Strickland if he asks. Or is this just a newspaper thing?"

"I'm investigating for an article. Yes." I sucked in a deep breath.

As our conversation unfolded, my doubts began to fade, replaced by a growing trust in Benjamin's integrity. However, the mystery of Emily's suspicions still loomed, and I couldn't shake the feeling that there was more to uncover.

"Benjamin, I understand that information has value, but I need to be certain that what you have to share is worth the cost," I said, my voice firm but tinged with curiosity. "Can you provide me with reasons why Victor might have had a motive to harm Graham? If the information proves to be substantial, I'm prepared to pay the fee."

Benjamin's expression turned contemplative, as if he was weighing the importance of sharing this knowledge. He nodded slowly and began to speak, his voice measured yet filled with conviction.

He looked at my bag as if I now needed to pay the two-hundred-dollar fee. This time, he didn't stop me from opening my bag and retrieving the cash.

"Victor and Graham were not just rival art dealers; their disagreements ran deeper. It all revolved around a painting—a forgery, to be exact," Benjamin revealed, his words carrying a weight of significance. "Victor had accused Graham of attempting to sell a forgery, a deceitful act that threatened both their reputations and the integrity of the art community.

"Victor was known for his meticulous attention to detail and his unwavering commitment to the authenticity of artwork. Graham's alleged involvement in forgery would have struck a blow to Victor's professional standing, potentially leading to financial losses and a tarnished reputation."

As Benjamin spoke, the puzzle pieces began to fall into place. The conflict between Graham and Victor had escalated beyond mere rivalry; it had become a battle of integrity and artistic authenticity. It seemed plausible that such a clash of ideals could have ignited a flame of resentment and fueled a motive for revenge.

Everything came back to what Hazelynn had mentioned about forgery. That made two people who mentioned forgery, which made me believe Graham was involved in fake art somewhere. How would I figure out what was a forged painting and what wasn't?

"There were heated arguments between them, accusations flying back and forth," Benjamin added, his voice carrying the weight of the revelations. "It was a clash of egos, driven by their unwavering dedication to their respective visions of art. Victor saw Graham's alleged forgery as an act of betrayal, one that he might have deemed worthy of a drastic response."

My mind whirled as I absorbed the implications of Benjamin's words. The forgery accusation presented a compelling motive for Victor to seek retribution against Graham, shattering their once-professional relationship and spawning a fierce rivalry.

"Victor vowed he'd never forgive Graham for the hell he'd caused him over this building." Benjamin caught my ear.

"This building?" I asked.

"Oh yeah. The village council shut down the gallery for an entire year because Graham told the environmental agency the building had some sort of asbestos and was sitting on some land that would harm the environment. I don't know. I was off on my yearly art retreat, traveling around the world painting gorgeous landscapes."

"When was this?" I asked.

"Two, three…" His eyes rolled up and back as he tried to recall the time period. "Not sure, but Victor lost a lot of artists who didn't want their paintings in a rotted-out building. As you can see, a lot of our paintings are in glass enclosures or a fair bit of distance from the viewing lines so the art won't be compromised. Each gallery has a very delicate air quality, and the smallest piece of bacteria can harm any piece of art, including sculptures."

I thanked Benjamin for his honesty, assuring him that I aimed to uncover the truth and bring justice to Graham's memory. As we continued our tour, our conversation took a lighter turn, returning to the realm of art and creativity. Behind it all, though, the lingering question of Emily's motives remained, fueling my determination to uncover the secrets that lay hidden within Holiday Junction's art district.

CHAPTER NINE

Benjamin had told me so much to think about. If what he said about his alibi was true, then he'd be off the list. Emily's list.

Even though he claimed he was with his artist friends, Emily put him on that list for a reason, and the answers to my questions would have to wait until I confronted her at the bar tonight.

But my questions about Cassandra Firbank wouldn't have to wait if she was in the Palette Café where Goldie said she'd be.

Passing by the picturesque streets, I noticed more charming eateries lining the sidewalk than just the Palette Café.

The aroma of freshly brewed coffee floated on the air, enticing passersby to indulge in a steaming cup of liquid inspiration.

"The Palette's Edge." I noticed a quaint art supply store that catered to artists of all mediums, offering a wide range of paints, brushes, canvases, and other materials to inspire creativity, based on the display window.

"Mosaic Dreams," I said, reading the sign of the captivating boutique.

I put my hands up around my eyes as I peeked into the window and saw the shop specialized in mosaic art. Intricately designed pieces adorned the walls and shelves. This shop celebrated the beauty of this ancient art form, from colorful mosaic tiles to handcrafted mosaic sculptures.

It would be a fantastic place to get someone a gift, but today wasn't the day for that.

Sculpture Haven was the next shop I passed. It appeared to be a gallery showcasing stunning sculptures in various styles and materials. Boasting everything from elegant marble statues to whimsical contemporary creations, this shop displayed the mastery of sculptors from near and far. Definitely different from Ceramic Celebrations located at the seaside, which was more for tourists and locals rather than sculptors to do pottery and clay.

"Oh," I squealed when I passed Artistry Blooms. I couldn't help myself. I loved a good bouquet of fresh flowers, and walking through the shop wouldn't take me any time.

Artistry Blooms was a floral bouquet with a creative twist, where imaginative floral arrangements were crafted like works of art, ranging from vibrant bouquets to intricate floral sculptures. This shop offered a fresh take on botanical beauty.

"Hello, let me know if I can help you with anything." The young woman greeted me as soon as I walked in. She was working with a customer but made sure she addressed me.

I nodded and smiled.

The fragrant embrace of nature enveloped me, transporting me into a world of vibrant colors and delicate aromas. The air was alive with the sweet scent of freshly cut flowers, their perfumes mingling and weaving an olfactory tapestry that awakened my senses. It was the most home-like smell I'd experienced since moving here.

The floral shop's interior greeted me with an explosion of colors, as if a painter's palette had come to life. Lush greenery adorned the walls, cascading down in a beautiful display of nature's grace. Pots of blooming flowers were scattered throughout the space, their vibrant hues captivating the eye and uplifting the spirit.

The arrangements were a sight to behold—masterpieces crafted by the florists' skilled hands. Bouquets of roses, lilies, and daisies stood tall in their glass vases, radiating elegance and charm. Each petal seemed to glow with life, capturing the essence of its natural beauty.

Some of the floral creations were artfully arranged in bouquet-style mesh, showcasing the delicate intricacies of the blooms. The mesh added a touch of modernity, creating a juxtaposition of the natural and the contemporary. Other arrangements were nestled in paper wrappings, reminiscent of gifts waiting to be unwrapped, their colors and patterns adding an extra layer of charm.

The balms of fresh blooms filled the air, a symphony of scents that mingled harmoniously. The sweetness of roses, the citrusy zest of daisies, and the delicate perfume of lilies blended seamlessly, creating a fragrant melody that danced on the breeze.

The florists moved with grace and precision, their hands carefully selecting each stem and blossom to create arrangements that were both visually striking and emotionally evocative. They expertly combined different flowers, foliage, and textures, ensuring that each arrangement was a work of art.

As I explored the shop, I marveled at the attention to detail. Colorful ribbons and decorative accents added the finishing touches, enhancing the beauty of the floral creations. The variety of plants, from small succulents to towering orchids, added depth and diversity to the shop's offerings.

Artistry Blooms was a haven of botanical wonder—a place where nature's artistry was celebrated and shared with those who stepped through its doors. It was a testament to the power of flowers to uplift the spirit and bring joy to the everyday. Surrounded by the vibrant colors and delicate fragrances, I couldn't help but feel a deep appreciation for the artistry that bloomed within those walls.

"Amazing right?" A woman sidled up to me and pointed at the fresh flowers I'd picked up. "And all from the mountains here."

"I had no idea such a lovely place was here, and I've been living in the village for a year now." I was embarrassed to even admit that.

"It's like our own little village up here. Time just stands still." She sighed and took the money I'd found in my bag to pay her.

"Time just stands still," I whispered. Her words sent an uneasy chill through my bones.

"I'm sorry, what?" she asked.

"Nothing. I'm Violet Rhinehammer, and I work at the *Junction Journal*. I'd love to come up here after the big Fourth of July festivities and see about doing an article on the shop." I was hoping she'd immediately say yes, but she didn't. "Well, here's my card if you decide to give me the pleasure."

On a normal day, I'd be thoroughly disappointed with her not agreeing to free press, but Graham was on my mind. So were the woman's words about time standing still up here.

I wasn't sure what she meant or why the words seemed to hit me so hard, but I knew I wouldn't forget them anytime soon.

With my bouquet in my arms, I passed a few more shops and took note of each one of them.

The Ink & Quill was a cozy bookstore and stationery shop I had to struggle to resist entering. All things related to journals, pens, and notebooks always got me excited, and like any bookworm, I wanted to browse the shelves, which were filled with literature ranging from classic novels to contemporary bestsellers.

I made a note to come back when I had more time to explore and hurried past the other shops until I spotted the Palette Café across the street.

A delightful symphony of aromas enveloped me as soon as I opened the door.

The air was filled with the rich, enticing scent of freshly brewed coffee, intermingled with the warm, buttery notes of freshly baked pastries. The sensory embrace promised a culinary journey of delight. Definitely a different vibe from Brewing Beans.

The café's interior greeted me with a cozy and inviting atmosphere. Soft lighting bathed the space, casting a warm and intimate glow. The walls were adorned with an eclectic mix of local artwork, creating a gallery-like ambiance that celebrated the fusion of art and culinary creativity. This place was certainly artsy.

The seating arrangements were a charming medley of vintage-inspired tables and chairs adorned with colorful cushions that added a touch of comfort and charm. The wooden floors creaked gently underfoot, hinting at the café's history and character. Small nooks with bookshelves invited patrons to relax and lose themselves in the pages of a captivating read.

Behind the counter, skilled baristas moved with precision, expertly crafting each cup of coffee with care and finesse. The gleaming espresso machine stood as the centerpiece, radiating an aura of creativity and craftsmanship. The sound of steaming milk and the gentle hum of conversation created a soothing background melody.

The menu, displayed on a chalkboard above the counter, boasted a tempting array of options. Artfully handwritten text described the tantalizing dishes for sale. From aromatic pour-over coffees to velvety lattes adorned with delicate foam art, the beverage choices were as diverse as they were enticing. The selection of pastries was equally alluring, with flaky croissants, moist muffins, and decadent cakes to tempt even the most discerning palates.

I joined the queue, eager to place my order and immerse myself in the palette of flavors that awaited. The friendly baristas greeted each customer with a warm smile, offering recommendations and engaging in lighthearted banter. The sounds of laughter and animated conversations created an ambiance of conviviality and shared enjoyment.

As I found a seat near the window, I saw that the view outside added to the café's charm. The street beyond was lined with vibrant flower boxes, bursting with colorful blooms that brought a touch of nature into the urban setting. Passersby strolled along the sidewalk, their laughter mingling with the gentle breeze that carried the scents of freshly cut grass and blossoming flowers.

I took a sip of my steaming cup of coffee, relishing the rich flavors that danced on my tongue. The blend was perfectly balanced, with notes of chocolate and caramel enveloping my palate. It was a moment of pure indulgence, a respite from the bustling world outside.

"Where have you been, Cassandra?"

I heard the name of the woman I'd been searching for and jerked up to see where the two people were. I watched as they talked.

Her dark, wavy hair cascaded down her shoulders, framing a face that held an intriguing mix of beauty and introspection. Her eyes, a mesmerizing shade of deep brown, contained a hint of sadness and wisdom beyond her years. There was a certain elegance in her poise, as if she carried herself with a silent strength tempered by the weight of secrets.

She dressed in a style that blended sophistication with bohemian charm. Flowing dresses adorned her slender frame, accentuated by delicate jewelry that whispered of her artistic spirit. Her presence exuded an aura of creativity, a certain ethereal quality that captured the attention of those around her.

After she got her to-go coffee, she walked past my table.

"Cassandra, excuse me," I interjected, catching her eye. "I couldn't help but overhear your conversation. I'm Violet, Millie Kay's daughter from the Leisure Center, and an employee at the *Junction Journal*. I have a few questions, if you don't mind."

Cassandra turned toward me, her gaze guarded yet curious. She nodded cautiously, and I gestured to an empty chair at my table.

"Would you mind joining me? I'd like to talk about Graham, your relationship with him, and perhaps uncover some answers." I pointed at the open chair.

Reluctantly, Cassandra took a seat, her expression guarded. I leaned forward, my voice gentle but filled with determination.

"Cassandra, can you shed some light on your relationship with Graham? Did you know why he was killed, or perhaps have any idea who would want to harm him?" I asked.

Cassandra's eyes flickered with a mix of emotions, her defenses slowly lowering. "Graham and I were once together, but it was a complicated relationship. We had our share of disagreements and secrets," she admitted with a hint of sorrow in her voice.

My curiosity piqued, I pressed further. "What secrets did Graham uncover? Was there something he discovered that could have led to his demise?"

Cassandra hesitated, her gaze fixed on the table.

"Graham... He had stumbled upon something, a secret that shook him to the core. It involved the art world, deceit, and the potential for irreparable damage to reputations. He was determined to expose it." She looked down at her to-go cup of coffee.

"Did it have to do with Victor Monroe?" I asked. "Did Victor know about the secret? Would Victor kill Graham over fear the secret would get out?"

Cassandra tensed up whenever I mentioned Victor's name. Her cautious demeanor suggested she understood the gravity of the situation, perhaps aware of the risks involved in sharing too much. Her evasiveness hinted at a deeper involvement or knowledge that connected Victor to the secret Graham had unearthed, which only fueled my curiosity even more.

I watched as Cassandra's guarded expression flickered with a mix of hesitation and apprehension. My inquiries were clearly treading upon delicate ground. Determined to uncover the truth, I leaned forward, my voice filled with earnestness.

"Cassandra, I understand the risks, but we need to know if Victor is involved in all of this," I implored, my eyes locked with hers. "Don't you want justice for Graham? You two dated for so long, and now he's gone. We owe it to him to find the truth."

Cassandra's gaze faltered, a hint of sadness flashing in her eyes. "Violet, I can't say any more. It's dangerous. Graham's death... It wasn't just a random act. There are powerful forces at play here, and I fear for my safety."

My heart sank as I realized the weight of Cassandra's words. Fear was gripping her tightly, suffocating any desire to reveal the full extent of her knowledge. Wanting to offer comfort and reassurance, I reached out, my hand barely grazing her arm.

"Cassandra, I understand your fear. But we can't let fear hold us back from seeking the truth," I pleaded, my voice filled with conviction.

"Graham deserves justice, and we need to uncover the secrets that led to his demise. Together, we can face this."

However, Cassandra's eyes widened with alarm. She hastily stood up, her chair scraping against the floor.

"I can't be involved anymore. I've already said too much," she said, her voice tinged with urgency. "I can't risk becoming the next victim. Please, Violet, let this go." Before I could respond, she swiftly gathered her belongings, clutching her bag tightly.

As she rushed toward the exit, a small card slipped from her bag and fell to the floor. I reached down to pick it up, and my eyes widened when I saw the name of the place where she worked—the very location where, according to Goldie, Cassandra worked various jobs during the summer months after school was out.

I put the card in my bag because I knew I'd venture back up here to possibly question her again. Maybe get an alibi once I talk to Emily and Victor. Or maybe to get the secret out of her.

As I watched Cassandra leave the café, my mind raced, connecting the dots. The forgery accusation against Graham, the rivalry with Victor, and now Cassandra's allusions to a secret within the art world. The puzzle pieces seemed to fall into place, and Victor's name continued to resurface.

CHAPTER TEN

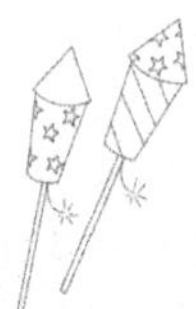

Not long after Cassandra left my sight, I noticed Benjamin Clarke exiting Gallery 360. For about one second, I debated whether to go back into the gallery and try to get information from someone besides Benjamin.

This time, I wasn't going to pay anyone for information. Or I could just get the information myself.

I gathered my things, took the last sip of the coffee I'd gotten, and headed back down the bustling street to Gallery 360. Like the rest of Holiday Junction, the art district wasn't spread out. From what I could tell, most of the shops were located within one little block. Also like the rest of Holiday Junction, the streets were crowded, which was good for me.

Slipping in and out of places was a skill I'd been able to hone over the last few years.

This situation proved to be no different.

The employees didn't seem to notice me in the crowd as I moved along with a few different groups, taking in the signs I'd not even bothered looking at an hour or so ago when I was here. I used each group to get closer and closer to the area where the signs read either Employees Only or Office.

Looking side to side with my eyes peeled, I slipped through a door marked Employees Only. I was shocked to see how much the atmosphere behind the scenes differed from the actual gallery.

The smell of fresh paint mingled with the scents of paper and cardboard, creating a distinct, earthy aroma that lingered in the air. Open cans littered the floor, as did paintbrushes, large canvases, and crates, some open and some closed.

The narrow hallway led me past several doors. If they were unlocked, I peeked my head inside. I found that behind each door hid secrets and treasures of the art world. The first door revealed a storage room, lined with shelves filled with art supplies, canvases, and frames of various sizes. The room exuded a sense of potential, as if waiting for the next stroke of creativity to bring these materials to life.

Farther down the hallway, a door swung open to reveal a small workshop. The room was cluttered with brushes, palettes, and an array of paints in every hue imaginable. Splatters of vibrant colors adorned the walls and floor, evidence of the creative process that unfolded within these walls. Canvases, some finished and others in progress, leaned against the walls, waiting to be showcased to the world.

Adjacent to the workshop, a door led to a modest office space, which appeared to be where some administrative tasks took place. Papers and files were neatly arranged on the desk, alongside a computer displaying digital records of the gallery's collections. The space held an air of organization and efficiency, suggesting that meticulous attention to detail was key there.

A final door opened to a small, cozy break room, providing a respite for the gallery staff. A round table sat in the center, covered with scattered coffee cups and a stack of art magazines. The walls were adorned with prints of famous artworks, creating an atmosphere of inspiration and creativity. No space was left that didn't scream art or the world created in Gallery 360.

There was no hint of an office for Victor, which made me wonder if he even had one. Or was there?

At the far end of the hallway stood a small door with nothing on it to reveal where it led.

For a moment, I stood still, trying to hear if anyone was coming or going before I took a chance and hurried to the door. As I did with the others, I slowly turned the knob, peeked inside, and saw a set of stairs. I had no idea where it went but decided to climb anyways.

The sounds of those scary movies started to play in my head—you know, the kind in which the dumb characters decide to go down the scary dark steps the killer is hiding underneath. The movies in which people walk straight into their untimely deaths as dark music plays in the background, causing the viewer's stomach to lurch with excitement and fright? That was exactly what I was feeling, and I ignored what could happen.

"Wow," I gasped when I got to the top and saw the most spectacular view of the mountains through the windows. Literally, I did a 360-degree turn like the name of the gallery and was awestruck at how gorgeous it was up here.

I snorted back a laugh and smiled when I realized this was Victor's office space.

The sunlight bathed the room in natural light, casting a warm glow upon the meticulously arranged furnishings.

The office reflected Victor's refined taste. A sleek mahogany desk stood at the center, adorned with a collection of antique trinkets and a carefully organized array of documents. On one corner of the desk, a framed photograph captured a moment frozen in time—a smiling Victor standing alongside renowned artists, their camaraderie evident in their expressions.

Bookcases lined the walls. Their shelves were filled with an assortment of art books and catalogues, showcasing Victor's passion for the arts. Sculptures, both intricate and abstract, were carefully displayed on glass shelves, captivating the eye with their intricate forms and craftsmanship. The room seemed to pulsate with the creative energy that emanated from each carefully curated piece.

The desk itself held a smattering of personal mementos—a photo of him with Mayor Paisley, a small keepsake from what looked like a memorable trip, and a vintage typewriter that hinted at Victor's appreciation for the classics. An item I would love to have in my office.

His office was definitely an amalgamation of artistic inspiration and personal touches, reflecting the depth and complexity of its owner.

Every detail within Victor's office spoke to his dedication to the arts and his status within the art community. This room was clearly not just a workspace but a reflection of his identity as an art dealer, leaving an indelible impression on all who entered.

Underneath a bookcase was a set of drawers. One of them was slightly open. I used the toe of my shoe to open it and saw a file stuffed in there with a few art magazines. That wouldn't have been unusual if not for the name Winston written across it in big red ink.

"What do we have here?" I asked.

Following my journalistic instincts, I picked it up and didn't care what the repercussions would be if I got caught. Which I did not plan to do.

"Here goes nothing." With bated breath, I opened the folder, revealing a wealth of information Victor had painstakingly compiled.

The pages were filled with damning evidence and shocking revelations about Graham's questionable practices in the art world. It seemed that Victor had delved deep into Graham's past, unearthing a web of deceit and manipulation that Graham had carefully concealed.

Photographs of forged paintings, detailed financial transactions, and correspondence with dubious individuals were neatly organized within the file. Victor had clearly been on the trail of Graham's illicit activities, amassing evidence to expose his fraudulent schemes.

As I studied the contents, my eyes widened in disbelief. The scale of Graham's deception was staggering, involving art forgeries, money laundering, and shady dealings with unscrupulous art collectors. Graham's dark side would definitely give someone a reason to have murdered him, but Victor?

What on earth could Victor's motive have been?

I gulped. What if Victor and Graham were arguing about all the things Victor had uncovered? Was this one of those cases in which the discussion got heated?

"Graham was going after Victor," I told myself as I looked out the windows over the mountains, never focusing on a single tree but instead on the images of the new theory.

My mind whirled with the implications of this newfound knowledge. Graham's actions had jeopardized the integrity of the art world, tarnishing the reputations of artists and collectors alike. No wonder Victor had been so determined to expose him and put an end to his deceitful practices.

"That's why Victor confronted Graham, and he had to defend himself or Graham was going to kill him."

I jerked around when I heard someone clapping.

"Victor."

"Wow. That's some sort of journalistic detective work. Kinda like those crime podcasts, but your accent makes it more like a joke." He walked over to me with his hand out, obviously wanting the file. "I was told someone stopped by to see me."

"I let myself in." I stood tall so he didn't see the shivering taking place inside me.

"I can see that." He continued to hold his hand out.

"I think I should keep this for the police." I curled the file against my body. "I can see why you'd have killed Graham."

"I heard your little theory on my way up the steps. I was thinking you were on the phone telling someone, but when I found you in here talking to yourself, I couldn't help but think it was pretty darn good." He ripped the file out of my hands. "But it didn't happen like that. I never got to talk to him. At least in the way I wanted to talk to him."

"Are you trying to tell me you didn't kill Graham Winston with all the evidence you have on him?" I pointed at the folder.

"Actually, I did talk to him downtown a while back." He shook his head and gestured for me to take a seat while he sat in his office chair. "I went to his gallery, if you want to call it that, and that's when Emily told me he was getting some coffees at Brewing Beans."

He was retelling his side of the story that Hazelynn had overheard and told me.

Anonymously.

So I didn't tell him I knew about it. I let him talk.

"Anyways, I went down to the coffee shop, and I was shocked to see the painting on the wall. I don't leave the mountains too much, and we have a fantastic little café down the road here for getting coffee."

"Palette Café." I smiled and nodded.

"I see you've been enjoying our little district up here." He grinned. "I think you're going to find it hard to leave."

"I will admit I was very surprised to see how neat it is," I said but quickly got back to the story. "Are you talking about the painting on the wall that resembles Holiday Junction?"

"Yes." Victor flipped the file open and shuffled through the papers before he settled upon one photograph. He took it out and turned it to show me. "This one."

"What about it?" I asked.

"The one he is trying to pawn off as the original is fake. A forgery," he said.

"And how do you know that?" I asked.

"Benjamin, who you met, is an artist. He has a very good eye for brushstrokes." Victor must've noticed I wasn't following what he was saying, so he began to break it down in my language. "It's like how every journalist has their own unique spin on how they deliver the news. Every artist has a different style or technique. Your questions covering a story might be different from the ones Marge Strickland might ask. The same with an artist. Two artists can be looking at the same tree, but when they start to paint them, they turn out vastly different. The way they stroke the canvas, hold their brush, mix the colors. Every little detail is different."

"And in this particular case, how do you know the one hanging up in Brewing Beans isn't the original?" I asked.

"Because we have originals from the artist and have been in contact with him several times over the year. In fact, we are scheduled to get the original of this exact painting in a couple of weeks," he said with confidence that he would be able to prove the piece's originality beyond a reasonable doubt.

"What about your argument with Graham?" I asked, knowing he might have me on the forgery piece, but in reality, I was there to try to uncover a motive for Victor to have killed Graham.

"I told him that he better stop trying to sell it. I also told him I had been in contact with the artist. But he refused to believe me. He said he had the original and it wasn't going anywhere. That we'd get the two paintings looked at and as far as he was concerned, there weren't any more paintings from this artist." Victor rolled his eyes. "We got into an argument."

"Did you kill him?" I asked point-blank.

"Why would I kill him over a forged painting? I have several originals about to go on display for when I get the seaside original. I'll have Emily use her keen eye now that I've offered her a job as my newest curator." He gave a little hint about why he might've been talking to Emily when I walked up on them. "If anything, Graham would have motive to kill me."

"Why?" I asked, wondering what Victor's line of thinking was.

"He didn't want me to expose him." He shrugged.

"Did you happen to argue with him the night of the fireworks and end up killing him in self-defense?" I asked, knowing it had to be some sort of self-defense if he went to the trouble of strangling Graham.

"No. I was right here in this office watching the fireworks from afar." He turned toward the other side of the office, where the view of the ocean was visible in the distance. "And Emily was here with me."

"Are you and Emily an item?" I asked.

"No. Graham was a workaholic. He also made sure his staff worked long hours like he did. Graham told Emily he was going to a meeting during the fireworks, and she had a moment to take me up on my offer to just listen to what I had to say. The only opportunity was during the fireworks." He shuffled through some of the papers on his desk and handed me another document. "You will find that is a contract between me and Emily. It's dated and time stamped and notarized by my attorney, Diffy Delk."

"Diffy does everyone's work," I commented and looked at the notary, which was dated and stamped for the time of the fireworks. That meant neither Emily nor Victor could have made it from the art district to the seaside in time to have murdered Graham.

"Someone else had a much bigger motive than I would have," he said and took the contract back.

"Emily is going to come work for you, then?" I wanted to make sure I understood all the facts before I left.

"She is. And we were going to tell you all this tonight at the bar, but here we are." He sighed and eased back into his chair, appearing satisfied with the outcome. "If you'll excuse me, I've got some work to finish."

"Then we aren't meeting for drinks later?" I asked to make sure.

"Unless you feel like there's a need, no. And honestly, I don't feel like coming off the mountain to go down there in that crowd. I'm not much for the Fourth of July. Now, give me an artist festival any day." He smiled.

"Has the Merry Maker ever held any sort of festival in the art district?" I wondered as I thought of a million different places up here.

"No. And we like it that way," he said before we bid each other goodbye.

"The Merry Maker hasn't yet," I whispered with a little knowing grin on my way down the stairs.

CHAPTER ELEVEN

Luckily for me, Goldie had gotten off work, and this shift's trolley driver wasn't as chatty as her, letting me regroup my thoughts for when I got back to the office. There, I found Radley and Darren.

"We've been waiting for you for a while." Darren greeted me with a kiss.

"I took an unexpected trip to the art district." My brows shot up. "I love it up there. Why haven't you ever told me how cute the shops and surrounding area are?"

"I guessed you were sick of the mountains and all the forest-type landscapes, considering where you moved from." Darren made a good point. "Why did you go up there?"

"To see Victor Monroe," I said. When Darren shifted uncomfortably, I continued, "I know I was going to meet him and Emily at the Jiggle Joint tonight, but after hearing the fight between Victor and Graham plus Graham and Cassandra's fight, I knew I could find Victor and Cassandra up there."

"Did you?" Radley asked, going straight into his journalism mode.

"Okay." Darren shook his head. "I can see you two are doing that intense work thing. I'm going to leave you to it. You aren't going to meet them at the bar?"

"No." That reminded me to get in touch with Emily somehow to let her know, even though I'd assumed Victor would do it.

"That means you are all mine all night." Darren vigorously rubbed his hands together. "Carnival rides and all." He sounded so excited as he left the cottage.

"So, what did you find out?" Radley was eager to get started. He beat me to the whiteboard.

"I'm not sure any of our suspects killed him," I said. "Let's go over Graham's profile one more time."

"Okay." Radley picked up the file from my desk. "Graham Winston. Fifty-two years old. Local art dealer."

"All we have on him is his occupation." I stared at the whiteboard, hoping it would come to life and tell me what I was missing. "He was strangled, which tells us it was a passionate murder. And he was meeting someone, which is rare."

"What?" Radley asked, shuffling through the file. "There's nothing in here saying he was meeting someone."

"That's what Victor told me." I quickly told him that Victor was able to seize the opportunity to woo Emily to come work for him and leave Graham.

"And the notary time stamp was during the fireworks?" Radley keyed in on that little detail, knowing it was virtually impossible for Emily or Victor to have been at the beach during Graham's murder.

"And I know the lawyer pretty well, so I can confirm with him." I knew it would be easy to get a confirmation from Diffy. "Graham Winston was a well-known figure and citizen, so maybe it had nothing to do with the immoral ways he ran the gallery."

"What about Cassandra?" Radley pointed at Graham's ex.

"I ran into her too. She was a little more scared." I tried to describe how Cassandra had begged me to leave her out of this case for fear she'd be next. "I couldn't get the secret out of her."

"Do you think she was refusing to answer because she killed him?" Radley asked.

"What if the secret was about her?" I wondered if we needed to look at her a little closer.

Radley must've liked the idea because wrote it on the board.

"Protection of a secret," I said. Then I elaborated. "Cassandra may have been privy to information or a secret that could have implicated her or others in unlawful activities. To safeguard herself and those involved, she might have felt compelled to silence Graham, who had discovered this secret. And that's what Goldie had overhead."

"Fear for personal safety because of Graham's mishandling of the gallery?" Radley offered another good motive. "She's in that world, and what if she isn't as clean as she appears?"

"She was saying she was in fear for her own life and even my safety." I made the point.

"Then let's go back to this secret." On the board, Radley had written "secret" under Cassandra's name and circled the word a few times.

"Loyalty and allegiance?" I asked, giving the idea a new spin. "Cassandra might have had a deep sense of loyalty toward someone involved in Graham's schemes?"

"She could've been on a date with him during the fireworks. That's the reason Graham took off work." Radley made several bullet points under her name.

"They got into an argument over the secret, and for self-preservation reasons, Cassandra could have had a motive rooted in aiming to protect her reputation, career, or personal interests." I threw it out there.

"It looks like we need to see Cassandra again. Make her talk. Get her alibi, if she has one," he said before Mama rushed into the office.

"Turn on the television!" she hollered, tossing the brochures on the desk. They skittered in all directions.

"Fine," Mama choked out.

Apparently, we weren't moving fast enough for her. She grabbed the remote, turning on the television herself.

On the television, Chief Strickland prepared to address the town in a live press conference. Too bad he didn't let me know so I could be there live.

He stood before a podium, exuding an air of authority.

"Ladies and gentlemen of Holiday Junction," Chief Strickland began, his voice steady and resolute. "I stand before you today to address the tragic incident that has shaken our peaceful community. It is with a heavy heart that I confirm the murder of Graham Winston, esteemed art dealer and cherished member of our town."

He continued, his words measured yet compassionate. "Our dedicated team of investigators has been working tirelessly to uncover the truth behind this heinous crime. Rest assured, we are leaving no stone unturned in our pursuit of justice."

He went on to tell the town, "While this incident is undoubtedly a tragedy, we have reason to believe it is an isolated incident. The safety and well-being of our residents remain our utmost priority, and I want to assure everyone that the Fourth of July festivities will proceed as planned. Holiday Junction will continue to embody the spirit of celebration and togetherness that defines us."

Chief Strickland's words carried a sense of reassurance, a reminder that the indomitable spirit of Holiday Junction would not be dampened by the events that had transpired.

As the press conference concluded, my mind buzzed with thoughts and questions. The weight of the investigation bore down upon us all, but knowing that Chief Strickland was at the helm, I had faith that justice would prevail.

"Mama, we'll need to talk to Cassandra," I said as I turned to Radley and Mama, their expressions reflecting a mix of concern and determination. We locked eyes, silently vowing to unravel the truth and bring closure to Graham's tragic fate.

As much as I loved my job, I had promised a night away so I could go with Darren to the carnival. Graham's murder wouldn't be solved by me or even Chief Strickland in the next few hours, so I let loose to enjoy my time with my new boyfriend.

"You're like a big kid," I teased Darren and squeezed his hand.

Darren and I strolled hand in hand along the picturesque seaside to the sounds of laughter and excitement. The Fourth of July carnival had transformed the beach into a vibrant wonderland, with colorful lights illuminating the night sky and the scent of cotton candy wafting through the air. The atmosphere was magical, and I couldn't help but feel a sense of childlike wonder as we immersed ourselves in the festivities.

"I want to experience it with you." He stopped and turned me toward him.

Darren's gaze met mine, his eyes filled with affection and mischief. He pulled me gently toward one of the food vendors, where the aroma of freshly popped popcorn tantalized me. With a smile, he handed me a bag of the warm, buttery delight, knowing it was one of my favorites.

"You've been to this celebration a million times." I didn't know much about his past, but I did know this wasn't the first Fourth of July Holiday Junction he celebrated.

"Not with you." He plucked a piece of popcorn off the top of my bag.

"Hey," I warned him, turning slightly away. "You've got your own."

As we meandered through the crowd, we laughed and shared stories, the joy of the carnival infusing our every step. The Ferris wheel loomed ahead, its gondolas glimmering in the night. Darren's eyes sparkled with anticipation as he turned to me, his voice soft and coaxing.

"Come on, Violet," he said, his voice brimming with excitement. "Let's take a ride on the Ferris wheel. We'll get a breathtaking view of the entire carnival from up there."

"Your lighthouse has spectacular views," I said, reminding him that he'd used the same tactic to get me up there.

"It's a Ferris wheel," he pleaded.

"It moves." I hesitated for a moment, a mixture of exhilaration and trepidation coursing through me. But his comforting smile and the twinkle in his eyes convinced me to take the plunge. With a nod, I let him lead me toward the towering structure, our hands joined and our hearts pounding in unison.

As we ascended on the Ferris wheel, the world around us transformed into a breathtaking vista of lights and motion. The night sky was a tapestry of stars, the distant sound of crashing waves mingling with the joyful shrieks of thrill-seekers on the carnival rides below.

With each gentle revolution, Darren's presence beside me felt like an anchor, grounding me amidst the whirlwind of lights and sensations. We whispered sweet nothings, our voices lost in the symphony of the moment, as the Ferris wheel carried us higher into the sky.

"Violet," he whispered in a voice filled with adoration, "being here with you, surrounded by the magic of this moment, feels like a dream come true. You bring light and joy into my life, and I'm grateful for every single day we share together."

Our lips met, and the anxiety I was feeling about being on the moving ride fell away, allowing me to really enjoy the moment.

The view was nothing short of awe-inspiring. The vibrant carnival spread out beneath us in a kaleidoscope of colors and sounds. The soft breeze carried with it the scent of ocean air, blending with the scents of funnel cakes and sizzling hot dogs from the nearby food stalls.

Time seemed to stand still as we took in the beauty around us. The Fourth of July fireworks exploded in bursts of color in the distance, painting the night sky with their dazzling displays. It was a scene straight out of a fairytale, and I couldn't help but feel grateful for this enchanting night spent with the one I cherished.

As the Ferris wheel gently descended, our feet touched the ground once more, and reality settled back in.

Hand in hand, we walked away from the Ferris wheel, the sounds of laughter and music trailing behind us. The night was still young, and there were more adventures to be had, but for that brief time, we had created our own world of magic and romance amidst the lively tapestry of the Fourth of July carnival.

CHAPTER TWELVE

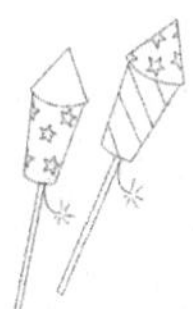

"I think we need to have the Merry Maker pick all the holiday spots at the beach," Darren joked after we'd entered the Jiggle Joint.

The place was packed.

"My goodness." I stood at the entrance and peered into the bar, where the old jukebox groaned and squealed tunes from the past for the people on the dance floor to scoot around to. "And to think you don't even have a show on the stage."

That was my way of telling him he really didn't have to run a jiggle joint to have a large crowd.

"Just think if there was a show." He wiggled his brows in a teasing way, his way of letting me know he had no intention of turning the bar into a respectable place.

I was greeted by a symphony of laughter, music, and clinking glasses. The air was thick with anticipation, and the room pulsated with energy. It was a Fourth of July extravaganza, and the bar was alive with merriment.

The jukebox in the corner blared out upbeat tunes, its melodies intertwining with the patrons' infectious laughter. The dance floor was a whirlwind of movement as couples swayed and twirled, their joyous spirits reflected in their bright attire.

The bar itself was a hub of activity, lined with patrons eagerly waving cash, waiting to order their favorite drinks.

As we made our way through the crowd, I couldn't help but notice the colorful spectacle that surrounded me. The patrons were decked out in all the Fourth of July regalia, proudly displaying their patriotism.

Red, white, and blue hats adorned with glittering stars, neon glasses with glowing frames, and cascading bead necklaces that shimmered in the dim light brought an element of festive whimsy to the scene. No doubt the festivalgoers had gotten some of the items from one of the vendor carts just outside.

The bar itself was transformed into a patriotic haven. Streamers in shades of red, white, and blue cascaded from the ceiling, while cutouts of sparkling fireworks adorned the walls. Miniature American flags peeked out of every available space, proudly proclaiming love for our nation. The bartenders' station itself was a visual feast, with a dazzling display of colorful cocktail ingredients and garnishes, tempting even the most discerning palate.

"Did you two throw up the Fourth of July in here?" I asked Owen and Shawn, who were still sitting in their same spots.

"Of course we did." Owen snorted and nodded toward Darren, who was walking around the bar, helping his employees with the crowd waiting to be served. "Do you think he was going to do anything?"

"You're right." I laughed because Darren never went all out on decorating for the holidays. He only fulfilled the bare minimum requirement from the Holiday Committee, and that was just to put up a display in the window.

Lucky for Darren, there were no windows in the Jiggle Joint, so he would pacify the committee members by taping something on the door to signify the holiday in question.

The energy in the room was infectious, a buzzing celebration of the holiday spirit. I joined the festivities, swaying to the music, occasionally catching glimpses of Darren behind the bar, his eyes lighting up with a shared secret between us. The night was filled with love, laughter, and the indomitable spirit of Holiday Junction.

Darren had gone behind the bar and filled Owen and Shawn's mugs and gave me a bottle of water.

"Excuse me," I said when I saw Emily sitting up front near the stage with a drink. Victor Monroe wasn't with her. "Hi, Emily," I said to her. "Is Victor here?" I asked in case he was in the bathroom.

"Not yet." She shook her head and picked up the small glass that held her cocktail. "I tried calling him, and he didn't answer. That's strange."

"I'm glad we have a moment to ourselves." I sat down next to her so I wouldn't have to scream across the table for her to hear me over the loud music.

"Yeah?" she asked.

"I actually went to see Victor today at Gallery 360."

My words appeared to make her nervous. She fidgeted in her seat before finally settling into position with one leg crossed over the other and both hands cradling the glass.

I continued, "He said he had asked you to come work for him."

"He did," she confirmed.

"Does that give him a motive to have killed Graham?" I couldn't help but ask. "I mean, if there's no Graham, there's no Winston Art Gallery, right?"

"It depends on what Graham stated in his will, I guess." She shrugged and took a drink. "You'd have to ask Diffy Delk those questions. I don't think Graham had enough time to change out his plans for the gallery."

"What plans?" I asked.

"His plans for Cassandra to come and work there," Emily said.

"Are you telling me Graham was going to give Cassandra part of the business? And that's why you have her on the list?" I asked.

"He said the art department at the school was getting a budget cut, and since Cassandra has her curator's degree already, she could easily step into the role. I overheard them talking about it at the beginning of summer, and she said she'd need part of the business, but then he said he wasn't ready to make the commitment but if it made her happy, then he'd do it." Emily shifted. "He had me make an appointment with Diffy Delk. A few days ago, Mr. Delk called the gallery and left a message for Graham. He said the papers were ready."

"Did he specify what papers?" I asked.

"No. When I told Graham about the message, he mumbled something about needing to change them again now that he and Cassandra were broken up."

Emily had just given me a definite motive for Cassandra. Had Graham made Cassandra part owner of the gallery? If he died, would that give Cassandra full ownership?

"You've not heard anything from Diffy or Cassandra since Graham's death?" I asked, so I could be armed with all the information before I went to see either of them.

Not that Diffy would give me any information. I was sure he wouldn't, but I bet if I went back to see Cassandra with enough nuggets of what Emily was telling me, Cassandra would have something to say.

"Nothing. But I'd been talking to Victor about a job because I'm just shy of my degree to be a curator and he said he was looking for someone." She looked around and then picked up her phone before placing it facedown on the table. I noticed some scrapes on her hands.

The little dots of dried blood were a sign the scrapes were pretty fresh.

"I don't know where he is. He's very punctual." She finished her drink and picked up the glass.

"What happened to your hands?" I asked.

"Work injury." She laughed, putting the glass back down, and stuck her hands in between the folds of her legs. "When you work in an art gallery, you get all sorts of scrapes and bruises."

"What do you know about Graham being accused of forgery?" I asked.

"Victor has been accusing Graham of it without any proof. Now that Graham is gone"—she gulped as if she had a lump in her throat—"he wants me to talk to the artists Graham had deals with to get them to move to Gallery 360. That's what he initially wants me to do."

"Can you do that without a curator's license?" I asked.

"No, but Victor said I could use his as his understudy and employee, though he'd have to sign off on them to complete the deal." She looked back again toward the door. "Really, I have no idea where he could be."

"What about Benjamin from Gallery 360? He was on your list." I wanted to question her about each name on the secret list she'd slipped into my hand.

"I saw him and Graham arguing, but when I asked Victor about it, Victor told me Graham had come to Gallery 360 and accused Benjamin of helping Victor. You know Victor has been accusing Graham of the forgery. In this business, if you get a bad name, you're out. No art dealer or buyer will do business with a curator if they believe they are selling forgeries."

"What would be Benjamin's motive?" I asked.

"Benjamin, like the rest of us, is also an artist, and when you're accused of something, you naturally want to defend yourself. Benjamin was right about the whole environmental thing." She opened the door for me to ask her a question about the month Winston Art Gallery was closed.

"You mean when Victor had Winston Art Gallery shut down?" I asked.

"Yes. It was awful and a bad move on Victor's part. Benjamin had told Victor it was bad for Gallery 360's reputation and that Graham was brilliant to move his gallery showing to Brewing Beans." She smiled. "I thought Graham was crazy when he said he wouldn't worry about Victor's scheme to get the gallery shut down because so many more people went to get coffee than came into the art gallery."

"Why did he think he could sell fancy paintings in a coffee shop?" I asked.

"Graham said common people, like those who didn't collect art…" She made sure she didn't offend me.

I smiled.

"Didn't really know they needed art until they saw something they liked," she said. "They'd never venture into an art gallery. They go to places like big-box stores to get poster-type art."

"So Brewing Beans gets lots of foot traffic, and the customers who linger in there get to actually see the paintings." I saw exactly how Graham's logical thinking really did work.

The painting hanging in Brewing Beans came to my mind immediately. I wouldn't go to an art gallery to purchase a picture to hang on my wall because I would assume I couldn't afford such a piece.

"When people see it in someplace like an everyday coffee shop where they're sipping their coffee like they would at home, then they see themselves at home with the picture, making the purchase much easier." Emily laughed. "Brilliant, right?"

"Yeah. It actually is. And Victor's little plan to have Winston Art Gallery shut down backfired." I snorted. "Why was the gallery shut down?" What had happened to cause such a repercussion was still unclear.

"That's why I have Patrick on the list," Emily said and picked up her phone again. "He is friends with Victor, and he's on the Village Developmental Committee. They have to make sure all the buildings in each area of town are built with the environment in mind. Since we have so many terrains and landscapes, there's a lot of hoops you have to jump through, and Graham had filed all the right permits for adding on to the back of the gallery to make it bigger. Victor had called on Patrick to check into it and sorta stall."

"Why would that make the gallery close?" I asked.

"Because when Patrick asked if Graham had gotten the soil tested and Graham finally did, it ended up coming back as something possibly bad. I don't know what it was, and the environmental agent they used actually closed down the building until they could take samples around the entire property. That's what took the month..." Emily's voice fell off. "I'm ashamed to say that's when I started to talk to Victor. I was afraid I wouldn't have a job, even though Graham continued to encourage me, saying I would."

She frowned. "I should've listened to him." She shook her head and picked up her phone again. "I have no idea where Victor is, and I've got to get up early in the morning to finish cataloging the art we do have at the gallery."

"One more question," I said and kept her there for another minute. "Why would Patrick want to kill Graham?"

"I wasn't sure, but I'd think a public fight where Graham threatened to make sure Patrick didn't get voted onto the committee again would be enough. Or the fact that Patrick felt like Winston Art Gallery should've been located in the art district." She shrugged and scooted her chair back. "I can't wait any longer. I'm not sure why he's not here, but I've got to go."

"Yeah. Sure," I said. "If he shows up, I'll tell him you had to go."

"Thanks. Violet, for what it's worth"—she stood up and then pushed the chair underneath the table to move it out of the other customers' way—"Graham really isn't any different than the other art dealers out there. They all appreciate art and want the world to experience what they see and feel. I guess what I'm saying is no matter what, Graham didn't deserve to die."

"I agree. I'm just trying to find some justice for him, and I think finding out the truth and reporting on it will help give our village some closure."

Emily walked away, and I followed her until she left the bar.

There were so many things she'd told me, but none of them pointed at a real killer, though the new information about Victor and Graham's history had gotten a little messier. It wasn't just what Victor was saying but also that he had pulled the development card.

"Happy Fourth of July!" a familiar voice behind me said.

"Happy Fourth." I turned to greet Leni and Vern McKenna, both of whom were decked out in matching Fourth of July outfits. "Did you make those?" I asked Leni.

She was the local tailor and could take any fabric, add a few stitches, and work her magic to make an amazing piece of clothing.

"I did. Doesn't Vern look great in this jacket?" She tugged on the edge of it before she ran her hand across his back, picking off some piece of lint.

"He does," I said, even though I wasn't sure Leni heard me because her attention had already shifted to another resident. They hollered at each other across the bar, and Lexi took off to talk to her.

"I hear you've been looking for me." Vern's bushy brow rose. "Darren told me."

"Yeah. I was wondering about your friend Graham, and you know." I frowned when I saw the look in his eye.

"Darren specifically said you were asking about Patrick. Patrick didn't kill Graham. They had their differences about the gallery location, but that was years ago." Vern pulled out the chair previously occupied by Emily and sat down.

"What about the environmental thing?" I asked.

He smiled. "He only did that because he had to. Whenever there's a report filed, they have to check it out. It just so happens there was some sort of mineral in the soil that ended up being nothing, but it didn't go without Graham being a jerk about it. Poor Danielle." Vern tsked.

"Danielle?" I asked.

"Yeah. The young lady who is in charge of doing all the testing for the company we used." Vern's eyes rolled back as if he was searching for something. Then he snapped his fingers. "Danielle Quillen!"

"Thanks. I might go see her." I made a mental note.

My phone chirped with a text. I pulled it out of my pocket and saw it was Louise. "I hope you have a great Fourth," I said to Vern and excused myself.

I thought I'd misread her text, but when I went over to the corner of the bar to open it, I saw I hadn't.

Get over to Brewing Beans!!!! Victor Monroe is dead!!!!

There weren't enough exclamation points in her message to compare to the shock resounding inside me.

CHAPTER THIRTEEN

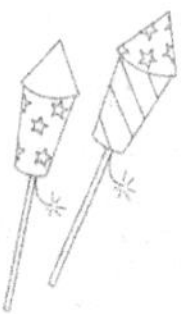

The sound of Louise's voice and news repeated in my head as I hurried down the seaside and up the path. Well, Darren and I hurried.

He'd seen my face when I got her text and he witnessed me bolt out of the Jiggle Joint without telling him where I was going or what news I'd just received.

Don't get me wrong. I was still on cloud nine from our date, and the warm breeze coming off the ocean felt good against my skin, making it one of those nights when sleeping on the beach would feel so nice. Plus the stars were out, and moonbeams flittered across the gentle ocean while the moon hung as far back as the eye could see.

Normally, it would be one of those nights.

But right now, my heart was pounding to the beat of my feet slapping the sidewalk, and Louise's voice made the melody a little more frightening.

Louise's voice had crackled through the phone, urgency ringing in her words after I didn't respond to her text. "Violet, you need to get over here. Brewing Beans. It's... it's Victor."

The weight of her words hit me like a sucker punch. Victor Monroe, the man I had planned to meet earlier that night, the prime suspect in Winston Graham's murder, was now... what?

"What happened, Violet?" Darren uttered.

"I don't know." My mind raced with the possibilities. "Your mom said to just get there. The phone line went dead as abruptly as it came to life."

Neither of us said a word as we started up the path leading to Celebration Park. I clutched Darren's hand a little tighter than usual.

"You're fine. We are fine," he assured me, knowing my sudden squeezing of his hand meant I was leery that the killer could be hiding in the forest on either side of the path.

We were met with the eerie sight of Holiday Junction as a ghost town draped in the aftermath of the day's Fourth of July celebrations. Streamers rustled in the breeze, their cheerful red, white, and blue colors mocking the grim reality of the moment.

The remnants of the day's festivities lay strewn about, the patriotic decorations fluttering in the warm wind, as if the town was stubbornly clinging onto the spirit of the holiday so it could hide the two deaths.

Brewing Beans was just a few shops away, but the way there felt like an eternity. The empty streets lay under the watchful gaze of the lampposts adorned with half-deflated balloons and bunting. The occasional firework exploded in the distance, a painful reminder of the day's joyous beginnings that had turned into a chilling nightmare.

The flashing lights of police cars and the coroner's vehicle near Brewing Beans painted an ominous scene.

"Did it happen in Brewing Beans?" Darren asked, his jeans making a swooshing noise as his legs rubbed together in our half-run, half-walk movements that took us closer and closer to the scene.

"I don't know. All she said was Brewing Beans, or at least that's all I heard." I noticed the shop's front window was shattered, shards of glass glinting in the harsh lights. My heart pounded in my chest as I approached, fear and anticipation gripping me.

As I crossed the threshold, my gaze landed on the lifeless form of Victor Monroe. The sight was chillingly similar to Winston Graham's murder scene. Victor's face was eerily calm, his eyes vacant, but the violent marks around his neck told a tale of a struggle, a desperate fight for survival.

The realization hit me hard—Victor Monroe hadn't killed Winston Graham.

He was strangled, just like Winston. Victor was supposed to meet me tonight, maybe to reveal something important about the murder. But now, he was dead, and the truth might have died with him. I could only hope that somewhere in this grim scene lay the clues that would lead us to the real killer.

"What are you two doing here?" Chief Strickland put his hands up, palms toward us, to try to get us to back up out of the coffee shop.

"I heard there was a murder. Victor Monroe," I said and popped up on my tiptoes to get another look at Victor's body.

"My wife?" Chief Strickland asked with a ticked-up brow. He shook his head at my silence. "We don't know anything."

"I do." I shrugged. "He was strangled just like Graham Winston, and he had to have come in here for that piece of art." I pointed at the wall. There lay a dusty outline of where the painting had hung.

"What painting?" Matthew asked.

"The painting!" Hazelynn gasped behind me.

I turned around to find her and Hershal standing on the sidewalk and looking into the broken front window. Hershal had left her standing there alone to talk to Matthew.

When I saw her standing stock-still on the sidewalk, my heart ached for her. She was staring into the shattered window of her beloved coffee shop, the flashing lights of the police cars reflecting off the shattered glass, painting a stark picture against the dark night.

"Hazelynn," I called out as I hurried over.

Her white nightgown fluttered against her legs, the hem speckled with dust and tiny shards of glass. She wore a hastily thrown-on faded blue robe over it, with her feet shoved into mismatched slippers. Her usually neatly combed hair was a wild mess, and her face was pale, her eyes wide with shock.

"Hazelynn," I repeated, more softly this time, placing a gentle hand on her arm. "Are you okay?"

She turned to me, her eyes welling up with tears. "I-I'm fine, Violet. Just... just can't believe this is happening."

I nodded, squeezing her arm gently. My gaze drifted to the empty space on the wall where a painting used to hang. Winston Graham had hung it there. That dynamic piece had become a fixture in the shop.

"Hazelynn," I began, my voice steady despite the chaos around us. "The painting that used to hang on the wall—do you remember anything about it?"

She followed my gaze to the empty space, her brows furrowing. "Winston hung that up. Said it was by some unknown artist. But... but he never told me the name. Why?"

"Did he ever mention anything about it?" I asked, pulling my notebook and pen out of my bag. "Anything at all?"

Hazelynn shook her head, her eyes flicking back to the shattered window. "No, he just said he liked it. That it added character to the place."

I jotted down her words, my mind spinning with possibilities. The painting, the artist, and now two dead men. I was missing a crucial piece of the puzzle.

"I'm sure you're in shock." I put the pen and paper away, knowing it was time to be a friend and not a journalist. "If you remember anything about the painting, can you call me?"

"Sure, honey." She nodded and raised her chin when Hershal walked back over.

"Matthew asked if he could see the cameras, and when I took him back there, the Fourth of July decorations were covering the only security camera we have." He shook his head, a defeated look on his face.

"Nothing they can see?" I asked.

"Not a thing." He frowned and put his hand on Hazelynn's back. "There's nothing we can do here tonight."

"I can't just leave it. It's our retirement." Hazelynn's eyes filled with tears.

"There's nothing we can do," Hershal repeated. "The police will be here all night looking for evidence. Possibly the next few days."

"Hershal is right," I assured her when I noticed her reluctance at his attempt to get her to leave. "I can promise you Matthew will do everything he can to get you back in the coffee shop."

"It's the Fourth of July and our biggest week every year." Hazelynn referred to the grim reality of living in a village where everyone relied on the tourists and their spending to make it through the year.

The shop owners didn't have lavish lifestyles, just comfortable ones. Something just like this could give them great financial difficulty.

The hum of an electric motor caught my attention, and I turned to see my mama puttering up the street in her golf cart. Despite the late hour, she was dressed as if she were about to host an afternoon tea party.

Her white summer dress, adorned with delicate blue flowers, was perfectly pressed without a wrinkle in sight. Her hair was coiffed in its usual elegant style. Not a single strand was out of place. Around her neck, a string of pearls gleamed in the intermittent flashing of the police lights, adding to her air of sophistication. Even at this ungodly hour, Millie Kay never left the house without looking her absolute best.

"Mornin', sugar," she drawled, even getting the middle-of-the-night hour correct.

She hopped out of the golf cart with surprising agility for the early morning hour. Her attention turned immediately to Hazelynn. Mama took in her disheveled appearance and the coffee shop's damaged facade.

"Oh, darling," Mama said, wrapping an arm around Hazelynn's shoulders. "I heard it on the police scanner. I'm so sorry, dear."

Hazelynn sniffled, leaning into my mother's embrace.

"I just don't know what we're going to do, Millie Kay. We can't open the shop during the investigation. It's going to hurt us financially." Hazelynn sniffed.

Mama patted Hazelynn's hand, looking thoughtful.

"Well, darling, I think I might have an idea." Mama always had an idea, so her reply didn't surprise me. "Tomorrow is the grand opening of the Leisure Center. How about you and your lovely coffee become our official guests? You can set up shop there, and we can put a big banner on the front of your shop, diverting customers to the Center."

Hazelynn's eyes widened, and a small smile tugged at her lips. "Millie Kay, that's... that's brilliant."

Relief flooded me, and I couldn't help but smile at Mama. Once again, she had come to the rescue, her southern charm and quick thinking turning a dire situation into an opportunity.

That was the way of life in Normal, Kentucky, where we were from. Mama had dragged all that southern hospitality with her, and even in the darkest of times, she showed the fine folks of Holiday Junction how to rally around one another.

It was the thread that held our little village together, the spirit that made us more than just a community—we were a family.

"I'll take care of this, and you take care of that," Mama whispered to me as she gave Hazelynn one last hug.

And Mama was going to make sure we all came together not only to help Hazelynn but also to find the killer before they struck a third time.

CHAPTER FOURTEEN

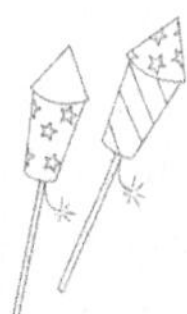

The sun was just beginning to peek over the horizon, the golden rays filtering through the window of my garage apartment. It was six in the morning, and the world was just waking, but I was already up and ready to face the day.

Ready to face more questions I needed to find answers to, now that two murders were concerned.

I quickly freshened up, pulling on a light summer dress and tying my hair back in a loose ponytail. Grabbing my bag, I stepped out into the fresh morning air, the scent of blooming flowers and dew-laden grass filling my senses.

My parents' house didn't look like anyone was up, so I slipped out of the side gate, knowing I'd be hearing from Mama sooner rather than later.

She'd driven me home last night after it was decided Hazelynn and Hershal would have a pop-up coffee shop at the Leisure Center. She also told me that I needed to write up a quick online article letting everyone know about the coffee shop and giving Mama's Leisure Center a little marketing.

Of course, I was happy to do so, but for now, I knew I needed to get to the office and write Victor Monroe's name on the murder board alongside Graham Winston's.

Just a few minutes' walk away lay the trolley stop. It was already alive with the hum of activity and the tourists' excitement about the last day of the Fourth of July Festival.

The day was filled with events all over the village and would end at the beach with a huge display of fireworks where the Merry Maker had placed the final sign. I hoped this time the explosion of brilliant lights wouldn't end with a dead body on the beach like the opening day had.

Goldie, the ever-cheerful driver, was at the trolley's helm, her eyes sparkling with excitement for the last day of the Fourth of July celebrations.

"Morning, Violet!" she called out as I climbed aboard. Her red, white, and blue outfit, complete with a star-spangled bandana, was a testament to her unwavering enthusiasm.

"Morning, Goldie," I said, taking a seat near the front. "Ready for the big day?"

"Oh, you bet!" she chimed, her hands gripping the trolley controls. "I'm off later this afternoon because Little Lizzy wants to go to the carnival, and I told her I'd take her."

"Oh, what fun memories." I sat back in the seat.

"Speaking of memories. Remember the other day when you and I were talking about Cassandra?" Goldie's voice rose above the rattle of the old trolley wheels and creaky metal windows.

"Cassandra?" I asked, my interest piqued. "Yes. Why?"

"She was on here earlier with Emily—you know, Graham's assistant," Goldie replied, her brows furrowed in thought. "It all seemed a bit... unusual. I've never seen those two together."

"Really?" My mind curled back to the night before, when I met with Emily. She'd kept looking at her phone and mentioning that Victor was never late.

"Her hands," I gasped. "Goldie! Stop the trolley!"

"What for?" She did it anyway. "We just got rolling."

"You just might've helped me solve the murder." So much glee filled me up that I threw my arms around her neck. "Have a great time with Lizzy, and don't forget to stop by the Leisure Center this morning on your travels so all these fine tourists can get some coffee from today's Brewing Beans pop-up shop."

I darted off the trolley, strapping my purse across my body as I took off running toward the police department. The trip was literally a three-minute jog if you went at a slow pace, something I could do and did.

"Are you sure you're okay?" Matthew eyeballed me as I stood inside the police department, bent over, hyperventilating as I tried to catch a breath.

"Emily," I gasped a few times. "Emily killer," I gasped again, taking the bottle of water he'd offered.

We both stood there looking at one another as I chugged down the water.

"Apparently, I should be in better shape," I was able to say without trying to grab some air. "But I knew I had to run here before you got started with your day and tell you something I just remembered."

"About the murders?" he asked to make sure. "I appreciate all of your help, but Violet, you're a reporter, and my wife is not going to fire you if you stop your little *Matlock* or—what is that British show she watches where they are on that island? We are not them. This is real life."

"I don't know what show it would be because I don't have that channel, but I do know when I see a clue, and when I see someone with scratches all over their hands before I go to a murder scene where the glass front window is shattered," I said and sat in the chair in this wide-open room that contained all the department's desks.

"Let's go to my office," he said, taking a vested interest in what I had to say.

"Finally." I sighed and pushed my tired legs to stand. They felt like spaghetti. I couldn't believe how I'd let myself go. I'd been living in Holiday Junction, where I walked practically everywhere.

Going into his office was fascinating.

"This is exactly like those shows you were just mentioning," I said, looking around at the boards bearing photos of all the people I'd been investigating. "Graham, Victor, Cassandra, and Emily."

I plucked her photo from the board and held it out to him.

"This is your killer." I let go when he took it. "She has motive."

Matthew looked at the photo and then back at me.

"Graham Winston's assistant?" Then he asked, "Why do you think she's the killer?"

"Emily had clear motives for wanting to kill Graham Winston." I paced back and forth as I told him the bullet points of what I'd found out. "She was getting her degree so she could be curator, but Graham had made Cassandra the beneficiary to his will, which Diffy Delk would know." I gave him that little tidbit so he could check it out. "And she gave me a list of people that would have motives for killing Graham."

I knew I was rambling, but I continued. "She gave me that list of bogus names to give herself time to get her story straight because she knew I would be chasing after the leads. Cassandra didn't do it. She had broken up with Graham because he had this secret, a secret I'm sure Emily knew. Then there was Patrick O'Connor. That was far-fetched." I continued to rattle off the list of names Emily had given me. "What about Benjamin Clarke?" I snorted. "She just wanted me to go to the art district to get me out of the village so she could meet up with Victor and solidify whatever little scheme they had going."

"You are doing a whole lot of mental chattering." Matthew looked a little frightened by my way of reasoning.

"I'm not even sure if Cassandra knew about Victor's death before today. The two of them were on the trolley this morning, and Goldie said she's never seen them together." I couldn't help but hear Matthew snicker underneath his breath, so I looked up at him. "Are you mocking me?"

"No. But you can't say that you and I killed someone simply because we are seen together or that you've become a deputy because you show up at all the crime scenes." He was pointing out that all of this was circumstantial and I needed more than just assumptions.

"What if I told you Victor had offered Emily a job? I can only imagine what Graham said the evening he was murdered. He probably told her, 'Fine, go,' and that's when she got angry, strangling the poor man." I was reaching for so many things that could point directly her at killing him. "Then Graham had a secret. Emily was his assistant. She knew all the secrets. Including that Graham had been accused of art forgery and that the painting that went missing from the coffee shop was one of Graham's. She and Victor were coming to some agreement, and they were supposed to meet me to tell me something last night, but only Emily showed up."

"Then she wasn't at the crime scene if you are her alibi." Matthew thought he had me on that one, but I hit him with the real, hardcore evidence.

"She did use me as her alibi. I clearly remember seeing all sorts of fresh scratches all over her hands. They had fresh blood spots on them."

That got his attention.

I continued, "I didn't even think about it last night after I saw Brewing Beans's shattered window and noticed that she kept checking her phone while we waited for Victor. He was never going to show up because he was dead. She killed him."

Matthew said, "I guess I could go take her in for questioning." He gnawed on the inside of his cheek. "Get some DNA from the scratches to see if it matches what we found at the scene."

"You found DNA?" I asked, knowing the usefulness of this evidence would depend on what types of tests they were doing and the time it would take to get those back.

"Yes, but that's off the record. I guess I'll walk down to the Winston Art Gallery." He was sure to let me know not to print his statements.

He walked to the door, and I followed right behind him.

"What are you doing?" he asked.

"I'm going with you," I said. "I won't be in the way. I just want to see how she reacts."

"You want the front-page story," he said. "My wife will stop at nothing to get a good story."

"Your wife is a brilliant woman," I said.

Vern had mentioned that the art gallery's location was Patrick O'Connor's problem. The gallery was just down the street from the police station, which was in an odd part of town because it included all the government buildings and the village's only hospital.

The area was known as Central Square. When we walked past the big concrete structure bearing the name, I wondered why Graham had picked this spot and not the art district.

Was it because of what Emily had said—Graham was good at his job of selling paintings because he let the work live among what we'd call the normal citizens? They'd see the art in their everyday lives and appreciate it for itself instead of the name on it or what type of medium the artist used. Art was a whole different world that I was probably never going to understand, but it wasn't so far removed that a criminal ceased to be a criminal. A motive of anger, greed, or whatever didn't deviate too much from one culprit to another, no matter what their occupation was.

The Winston Art Gallery was closed due to the nature of the hour. It was still early, and another couple of hours would pass before the gallery opened.

But it sure did open when the chief of police knocked on the door.

"Chief Strickland." Emily gulped, looking surprised. "Violet."

She held the door tight to the side of her face.

"What are you two doing here so early?" she asked. I couldn't help but notice her hands, and I was right—the scratches were still there.

"Do you mind if we come in?" Matthew asked.

"I'm sorry. The gallery isn't open right now." She shuffled a little to try to cover up our view as Matthew and I tried to see around her. Then I noticed some commotion behind her inside the gallery.

"Is that Diffy Delk?" I asked. "Diffy!" I yelled over her.

Ahem. Matthew cleared his throat and had me step back a few feet.

"Either you can let us in or I can call the judge right now to get a warrant." His voice was commanding.

"Can you hold on for just a second?" She must have not really wanted his answer because she shut the door, leaving us outside on the sidewalk.

A couple of minutes later, Diffy Delk opened the door for Matthew and me.

"Diffy, just the man I need to see." My brows rose. Out of the corner of my eye, I saw Matthew looking at me.

"I didn't know you were working for the Holiday Junction Police." Diffy had always commanded a big presence when he was in a room.

My eyes couldn't help but be drawn to his distinct appearance. He wore a toupee that perched precariously on his head, its deep hairline accentuating the artificiality of his hairstyle. The strands appeared unnaturally thick and perfectly arranged, giving him an air of pretense.

Diffy's choice of attire matched his slightly unscrupulous reputation. He dressed in garishly colored polyester suits, as if trying to use boldness to compensate for a lack of style. The fabric clung to him in a way that suggested both discomfort and an attempt to appear more sophisticated than he truly was.

His face wore a perpetual slick smile, adding to his smarmy demeanor. He seemed ready to charm or deceive, his eyes glimmering with a mix of mischief and self-interest. Every movement he made, from the way he adjusted his tie to the calculated tilt of his head, exuded an aura of calculated cunning.

Clearly, he was a man who thrived on the art of manipulation. His appearance, with the telltale toupee and polyester suits, formed a visual representation of his willingness to bend the truth and cater to his own agenda.

As our eyes briefly met, I couldn't help but feel a shiver down my spine.

I'd never been on this end of the relationship. I'd gone to Diffy for not only personal legal issues but also professional ones. Only this time, I was accusing his client of murder, and thanks to the way he was portraying himself, the air in the room held a sense of unease, as if his deceptive nature was contagious.

His involvement on Emily's behalf obviously held the potential to further complicate the already tangled web of secrets surrounding Graham's murder.

"Hey, Matthew." Joaquin Camsen walked into the gallery from the open door. "Violet, Diffy." He nodded as he greeted each one of us. "Emily." He grinned.

"Joaquin, someone else I need to see," I stated with satisfaction. Then I was caught off guard when Cassandra walked from a back room in the gallery to join us.

"Violet," she said, greeting me with a different attitude than she had yesterday.

"Cassandra." Seeing her standing there shocked me to my core.

"I'm guessing you're surprised to see me." Her eyes danced as though my reaction had delighted her.

"I'd heard you two were on the trolley, and that's when I knew I had to take all my information to Matthew—um, Chief Strickland." I gulped and decided it was time to take my chance at solving Graham and Victor's murders.

I walked around and drew in a big deep breath, gathering my wits and confidence at the same time.

I stopped.

I turned around to face everyone.

I stood in the middle of the Winston Art Gallery, surrounded by an uneasy silence. Chief Strickland, Diffy Delk, Cassandra, Joaquin, and Emily all stood before me, staring at me with a mixture of curiosity and trepidation. It was time to lay out the motives, to connect the dots, and to shed light on the truth that lay hidden in the shadows.

Taking a deep breath, I began to speak, my voice steady but laced with an undercurrent of determination. "Chief Strickland, Diffy, Joaquin, Cassandra, Emily... It's time to face the motives that lie at the heart of Victor and Graham's murders. Motives that drove not one but both murders."

Chief Strickland raised an eyebrow, his gaze steady as he leaned forward, waiting for me to continue. Diffy, with his slick smile, seemed intrigued, while Cassandra and Emily exchanged nervous glances.

I turned to Cassandra, my voice firm as I laid out the evidence. "Cassandra, you had a motive to kill Graham. Your relationship with him was tumultuous, and you were no stranger to his shady dealings. You feared that he would expose your involvement in his schemes, tarnishing your own reputation as an artist. You wanted to protect yourself and your future."

Cassandra's eyes darted around the room, guilt and fear playing across her face. She opened her mouth to speak, but the words caught in her throat.

Turning my gaze to Emily, I continued speaking, my voice measured. "And Emily, your motive was not just for Graham's murder but Victor's as well. You were Graham's loyal assistant, always in the background while he soaked up the spotlight. You resented his success, the way he took credit for your hard work. Killing him meant stepping out of his shadow, reclaiming your own talent and recognition."

Emily's face contorted with anger and desperation. Her voice shaking, she interjected, "You don't understand, Violet! It's not what you think!"

But I pressed on, determined to lay bare the truth. "The evidence indicates a deeper connection between both murders, a secret they shared. Graham had discovered something, something that threatened not just Cassandra but also Victor. It was a secret that would expose their collusion and fraudulent practices." I pointed at Cassandra. "Cassandra was going to take over the art gallery, which would put Emily out of the future she thought she had, but Cassandra had secrets about Graham, and Emily knew she could use them to expose the forgeries, tarnishing Cassandra's reputation from the get-go."

I twirled around to look at Emily again.

"We all know that your reputation is all you have in the industry." I clasped my hands in front of me and continued, "That's why the two of you are here today. You both knew you had to have one another to be a great success. So the two of you came up with a plan to kill both men."

Silence settled over the room as the weight of the revelations sank in. I could feel the tension thick in the air, the emotions simmering beneath the surface. There was so much more to uncover, so many loose ends to tie up.

As I looked at Cassandra and Emily, I saw the flickers of guilt and fear in their eyes. They knew that the walls were closing in, that the truth was catching up with them.

It was up to Chief Strickland and the justice system to determine their fate, but I had played my part in unraveling the tangled web of motives and secrets.

"Is this all true?" Matthew asked.

"Some parts but not all." Diffy Delk's mouth leveled into a tight grin I knew very well. "And I'll be more than happy to clarify everything Violet is accusing my clients of."

"Let's hear it." I tossed my hand up in the air, wiggling my fingers.

"May I?" Cassandra asked Diffy. He nodded.

"You're right," she said. "I did know Graham was harboring a big secret. As you know, I am Holiday Junction's art teacher. Over the years, I've had many students. As you can imagine, there's a lot of art going on and left behind. A couple of years ago, I had to switch classrooms, and Graham was helping me. He asked me about a few of the paintings, and I told him I had no idea who did them. They were just left behind."

Cassandra spoke with ease and confidence about her story and history with Graham.

"We were happy. I thought we were happy until I came to the art gallery and saw a couple of the student paintings hanging up in here with names I didn't recognize. They were paintings that were supposed to be thrown away when I moved classrooms." Her face stilled, and she looked off into the distance like she was watching the scene play out in her head. "I don't spend a lot of time in the village. Most of my time is spent in the art district, and there was a painting in the coffee shop..." Her voice trailed off.

"The painting was by a student?" I asked.

"Yes. It was another student painting. I couldn't believe it. It had the same fake name as one of the others in the gallery. It was at the end of the school year, and we got into a very heated argument about it. I told him it was a forgery, and he couldn't put my student's art on display. Not only could I get fired and go to jail, but he certainly would if the student recognized the art."

I looked around and saw we were all mesmerized by the tale.

"I told him I had to break up with him and couldn't date anyone who would do such a thing. He told me he would take them down, and he did, but he didn't remove the one in the coffee shop. I'm guessing he thought no one would really pay attention to it until he got a huge offer from an art client." She gestured to Emily.

"That's where I come in," Emily said. "Graham had me call Cassandra and try to talk her into letting him sell the piece. That's when I knew he had still decided to give Cassandra the gallery if anything happened to him as his way of making things right with her. If something did go wrong with the forgery, Cassandra might get fired, but she would have the gallery to fall back on for income, and she could easily disguise her involvement as the owner if she hired the right curator." Emily brought the secret Graham knew to life.

"But I didn't and don't want the gallery," Cassandra added. "I want the artist to come forward if possible, and that's what we were going to do. Victor was willing to take the gamble on his reputation and help us find out who the anonymous client was by letting them know it wasn't for sale. Then, Victor, Emily, and I were going to see if we could get the painting from the coffee shop or even somehow take a photo to plaster all over social media to find the true artist. I'm not sure what happened, but my fear is Victor was going to the coffee shop to meet someone he'd gotten in contact with about the painting and things went south."

"And that's when he was killed." Emily's voice choked. "Last night, when we were meeting you at the bar, we'd planned on asking if you'd do an article in the newspaper about the painting in the coffee shop. Help us get the word out and find the artist. I knew he had found something out about the painting because when we were talking on the street while you saw us, Benjamin had called him to let him know someone had called back. Victor didn't tell me who or the details, just that he was going to have a quick meeting with whoever it was. The next thing I know, we are all standing here with two dead art dealers and fingers pointing at us."

"As you can see," Diffy said, "my clients were not involved in killing anyone. They were trying to make sure all of Graham's forgery pieces were actually going to be truly certified by the rightful artist." Diffy talked in art-industry terms and legalities that I didn't need to know or bother to concern myself with.

All I knew was these two women claimed they had nothing to do with the murders and I'd just completely accused them of the horrific crime.

"What about your alibis?" I asked.

"That's where I come in." Diffy tugged on the edges of his shirt, exposing the tarnished cuff links. "The two ladies contacted me right after Graham was murdered, thinking these paintings were a motive for his murder. Little did they know Graham and I had met and he'd given me some information about the painting hanging up in the coffee shop."

"What is the information?" Matthew asked.

"You see, it's client confidentiality, but now that there's two murders, I will disclose he was getting death threats about the forgery painting. Apparently, the artist did learn the painting was in the coffee shop. He'd told Graham to meet him at the beach on the night of his death. Graham and I had a plan to get the painting to the artist. Unfortunately, I'm not sure what took place at their meeting for the artist to have killed him." Diffy had the best information of all of them.

"You didn't come to the police with the information?" Matthew asked. "And now two people are dead."

In no uncertain terms, Matthew put Victor's blood on Diffy's hands.

"That's not fair, Matthew." Diffy pointed a direct finger at the chief. "I was going to come to you with all this information. In fact, I was here this morning talking to my clients so we could form a game plan for coming to the department now that two art dealers are dead."

"Graham Winston and Victor Monroe," I stated. "The two art

dealers have names. Besides, the front window of Brewing Beans was busted out, which makes me wonder how Emily got those scratches on her hands."

On instinct, everyone immediately looked at Emily's hands. She held them out with a deep laugh as if it was the most ridiculous thing she'd ever heard.

"That's good!" She couldn't contain herself. Now she was hyperventilating with laughter.

"Can you tell us how you got the scratches?" Matthew asked.

"Tell you?" She giggled. "I can show you."

We all followed her through the gallery and into the back room where Cassandra had come from. Like Gallery 360, this room contained all sorts of paint cans, easels, and paintbrushes thrown all over the place as well as other art media.

Emily walked over to a tarp that held large pieces and small shards of glass in red, white, and blue tints. This canvas had a few pieces of glass glued onto it and was turning out to be a piece of art.

"I'm an artist. I work with glass, and my hands are always chewed up by the sharp pieces. Yesterday, I worked all day because it's what I do when I'm stressed, sad, depressed, or even happy. Graham's death has hit me hard. He might've been a little shady, but he was a great friend and boss. I'd never, ever kill him." Emily stared at me, her nose flaring as her passion about the relationship she'd had with Graham Winston was exposed.

"You didn't even need to say that much," Diffy said. He walked over to comfort her. "My clients both have alibis. Emily had come to see me right before she met with Violet at Brewing Beans, which was just before Hazelynn closed. I went there to see the painting in question. I even dropped her off at the bar to meet Violet. Cassandra was at the school. After she got off work at her café job, she went to school to once again switch rooms."

"I don't have a lot of free time during the summer days because I have to have a couple of jobs to pay my bills in the summer, so I need to change rooms at night when I'm not working," Cassandra said. "The janitor from the school let me in, and he was there with me, so he can tell you I was there." Cassandra looked directly at Matthew.

No sooner did Cassandra and Emily finish their story than Matthew dragged me out of the Winston Art Gallery.

"I can't believe I listened to you. Not only did you just accuse two women who look to have solid alibis, but you made me look bad. Let the investigation unfold with real evidence. Real police work. Not overhearing an argument here and there, scratches on hands, and all that." He threw his hands up in the air and stalked off down the sidewalk.

"There's still a killer on the loose!" I yelled.

"You stay out of it!" Swiftly, he turned around and jutted a hard pointed finger at me. "Or I'll arrest you!"

"We'll see about that," I said under my breath, wondering when Matthew Strickland would realize staying out of these situations wasn't so easy for me to do.

There was one person I remembered hearing them mention—Benjamin. Benjamin had notified Victor that the artist had called. I wasn't even sure if Matthew picked up on that. But this journalist here did, and that might be the key to finding out who killed Graham and Victor.

That meant I had to go back up to the art district and see if Benjamin would give me any information on the mysterious caller who set up the death meeting with Victor.

CHAPTER FIFTEEN

By the time I texted Radley about the online paper—luckily for me, he was very intelligent and had used the same newspaper publishing system as we did years ago, though he did grunt a little that Holiday Junction was in the Stone Age—he was able to list all of the Fourth of July festival's final events. He also listed the paper's newest sponsors so he could publish the edition for me.

"You know, you can do all of this ahead of time," he told me in a little bit of a frustrated tone. "But I'm not in charge. I'm just letting you know."

"I don't think I'm in charge, either, but before you—" I could hear the frustration in my own voice and didn't want to scare him off, so I decided to bite my tongue. "You know..." I sucked in a deep breath to dampen down my ego and pride. "You're right. I think you and I can come up with a great strategy to work more efficiently."

I could've rambled on and on about how I'd restored the *Junction Journal*'s respectability over the last year and that taking a willy-nilly approach to publishing wasn't always how I did things. However, due to the body count, which had climbed to two, cooperation was how I rolled.

"Really?" He sounded a little shocked. I could even picture his face from the other side of the phone, and I smiled.

It actually made him happy.

"Really," I said, feeling like it wasn't so bad to dampen my feistier side when that side wasn't necessary.

I'd save that for Benjamin if he gave me any pushback on what Cassandra and Emily had told me or tried to withhold any information.

The next trolley going up to the mountains to the art district seemed like it took forever. My stomach was growling. I'd yet to get my cup of coffee or even something to eat.

After the trolley trudged up the hillside, giving me some time to read the online edition of the *Junction Journal* Radley had published, my first stop was Gallery 360.

It was closed until ten a.m.

In fact, when I twisted around, I realized the streets were practically empty. I decided to stroll down the sidewalk and do a little window shopping. I had about an hour until the gallery opened, and I certainly wasn't going to go back down into the village.

Not too far down from the gallery, I noticed a small sign on a shop window that flashed Open. I couldn't make out all the words on the front of the door, but I did notice one. Bakery.

My stomach growled and got louder as I darted across the street as if a car were approaching. Nothing was coming. Not a soul. Not a car or even a critter.

"Sugarbrush Bakery," I said with a grin. "How charming."

I pushed open the door to Sugarbrush Bakery and was immediately greeted by a cool and inviting ambiance that enveloped the air. The bakery had a hip and artistic vibe, with its exposed brick walls adorned with colorful murals and shelves displaying whimsical knickknacks. Soft jazz music played in the background, setting a relaxed and creative tone.

The scent of freshly baked pastries filled the air, a symphony of warm butter, vanilla, and toasted sweetness. My eyes were drawn to the display counter, where a stunning array of artfully crafted pastries beckoned me closer. Delicate cupcakes topped with intricate fondant designs, sugar cookies shaped like tiny masterpieces, and macarons in an array of pastel hues were displayed like edible works of art.

As I took in the delightful scene, a vivacious figure emerged from the kitchen.

"Welcome to Sugarbrush Bakery, darling! I'm Amelia Hartman, the owner and artist of these fine pastries," she exclaimed with a warm smile. "What brings you to our sweet haven of artistic delights today?"

Amelia Hartman was the creative force behind Sugarbrush Bakery. Her lively red curls framed her face like an artist's brushstrokes, and her eyes sparkled with a mischievous twinkle. She wore a retro-inspired apron patterned with sugar brushes, showcasing her playful personality.

I couldn't help but be captivated by Amelia's infectious energy and her passion for her craft. Her dedication to turning pastries into art was evident in the bakery's every detail.

Sugarbrush Bakery was clearly a reflection of her unique artistic vision.

"Amelia, your bakery is a true feast for the senses," I said, my voice filled with admiration. "The pastries here are not only visually stunning but also taste as delightful as they look. It's a true testament to your talent and creativity."

Amelia beamed with pride, her eyes shining with artistic inspiration.

"Thank you, my dear! Each treat at Sugarbrush Bakery is lovingly crafted with a touch of magic and a sprinkle of whimsy. We believe that art and sweetness go hand in hand, and it brings me joy to see people savoring the beauty of our creations." She looked at another employee who'd come out of the back with a trayful of donuts that weren't just donuts. All sorts of things were stacked on top of them. Glaze was drizzled over them, and they looked just plain yummy.

I returned Amelia's warm smile, feeling instantly at ease in her whimsical presence. "I'm Violet, a journalist at the *Junction Journal*," I introduced myself. "I couldn't resist the temptation of your artistic pastries. They're absolutely stunning."

Amelia's eyes twinkled mischievously. "Ah, a journalist! How thrilling! Tell me, Violet, have you discovered any scandalous secrets in our dear Holiday Junction?"

I chuckled at her playful remark. "Not yet, Amelia, but I'm always on the lookout for intriguing stories. And as for my hometown, it's actually called Normal, Kentucky. Can you believe it?"

Amelia's eyes widened with curiosity. "Normal, you say? How delightful! But, darling, there's nothing normal about Holiday Junction, is there? We're a town of eccentric characters and thriving creativity. Especially up here in the art district."

I laughed, nodding. "You're absolutely right, Amelia. Holiday Junction is anything but ordinary."

Amelia obviously hadn't heard of me or how I had made Holiday Junction my home. I decided not to tell her.

Her expression turned mischievous as she leaned closer. "Well, Violet, I must admit, we like to keep things wonderfully peculiar here. We don't settle for normal—we embrace the extraordinary."

I couldn't help but grin at her infectious enthusiasm. "That's what I love about this town, Amelia. It's a haven for artists, dreamers, and those who dare to be different. And your Sugarbrush Bakery is the perfect embodiment of that spirit."

Her eyes sparkled with pride. "Thank you, Violet. It warms my heart to hear that. Sugarbrush Bakery is my little contribution to this wonderful tapestry of creativity. Each treat I create is a small piece of edible art, crafted with love and a dash of eccentricity."

Once we continued our conversation, we discovered shared interests and a mutual appreciation for Holiday Junction's unique charm. We enjoyed a delightful exchange of stories and laughter, fueled by the enchanting ambiance of Sugarbrush Bakery and the delectable pastries that surrounded us.

Every once in a while, someone would come in and get a donut and a coffee to go, but Amelia's employees took care of them.

Just then, it felt as if I had found a kindred spirit in Amelia, someone who understood the magic and quirkiness of this extraordinary town. Savoring a bite of the artfully crafted donut she offered, I couldn't help but feel grateful for the unexpected connections and moments of joy that Holiday Junction had brought into my life.

As I listened to what she told me, her passion for art and baking became even more apparent. Her love for her craft radiated from her every word and gesture. Clearly, Sugarbrush Bakery was more than just a place to indulge in delicious pastries—it was a harbor for creativity, a sanctuary where artistry and flavors intertwined.

I'd bet money that her presence and vivacious spirit made Sugarbrush Bakery what it was, even though the pastries looked and tasted wonderful anyway.

She had a special touch that made me want to come back.

As I stood at the counter of Sugarbrush Bakery, savoring the delectable flavors of Amelia's pastries, she looked at me curiously. "Violet, my dear, why are you here when you should be covering the Fourth of July festival? Isn't that the journalist's duty?"

I chuckled softly, knowing that her curiosity was well-intentioned. "You're absolutely right, Amelia. The festival is a big event, but I actually have another reason for being here today. I'm on a personal mission, you could say."

Her eyes sparkled with intrigue. "Oh, do tell, Violet. I'm all ears. What's this personal mission of yours?"

After taking a moment to compose my thoughts, I leaned in closer to Amelia. "I'm heading to Gallery 360," I confessed, my voice hushed. "There's something there that I need to uncover, something related to the recent events."

Amelia's expression shifted, her eyes widening in understanding. "Ah, the gallery," she murmured. "I had a feeling you would eventually find your way there, my dear."

Surprised by her response, I leaned back slightly. "You knew about Victor? Why didn't you mention it earlier?"

She offered a knowing smile. "I didn't want to scare you off, my dear. Victor Monroe is a complex character, and I didn't want to cloud your judgment before you had a chance to uncover the truth on your own."

I nodded, appreciating her thoughtfulness. "Thank you, Amelia. That means a lot to me. Now, what can you tell me about Gallery 360? Do you know anything that might help me in my investigation?"

Amelia paused, her fingers tapping thoughtfully on the counter. "Gallery 360 has been a prominent fixture in the art district for years," she began. "Victor is known for his eclectic taste and unique approach to art. But beneath the surface, there are whispers of shady dealings and hidden motives. Rumor has it that Victor is not afraid to cross ethical boundaries in pursuit of success."

My interest piqued, I leaned in again. "And Graham? Did he have any connection to Victor's world?"

Her eyes darkened momentarily. "Graham Winston was a talented artist and a complex individual," she replied. "There was a time when he and Victor shared a close bond, but something happened. Something that drove a wedge between them. Only they truly know the depths of their relationship and the secrets they held."

As I absorbed Amelia's words, I realized that the gallery held more secrets than I had initially suspected. Victor Monroe and Graham Winston were entangled in a web of intrigue, and it was up to me to untangle it. With Amelia's insight, I felt a glimmer of hope that I was getting closer to the answers I sought.

But as I looked into her eyes, I couldn't help but wonder if she held more knowledge than she let on. She had a depth, an understanding of the intricate workings of the art district that intrigued me.

I couldn't help but feel they all had one another's backs up here and no amount of coaxing from me would convince her to give me any information.

"Well, I'm actually hoping to find some breaks in the case and find justice for the men, no matter why they were murdered." I took a business card out and put it on top of the counter. "If you hear anything, I'd really appreciate a call."

"Sure thing, doll." Amelia picked up the card and looked at it. "I love the name Violet. I actually love popping little violets on top of cakes. It's colorful, and I think you are colorful."

"Some say I was a bit feisty, but since living in the village, I think I've kinda calmed down." I hated to admit it, but I did feel like I'd gotten a little soft.

"Then you need to move up here. You're a writer. An artist. You belong in the art district," she said and flailed her hand in the air. "There's some cute little apartments above these shops that you could rent."

"I appreciate that, but I actually live in my own apartment on my parents' property on Heart Street." The thought of moving up here was tempting, but visiting would be fine for now. "Anyways, I'd love to do a story on your bakery for the paper during a lull month. And by that, I mean when there's not a holiday that takes all my time to cover."

"That would be wonderful, honey." She finished all of her sentences by calling me "honey," "dear," "sugar," and similar names, even though we were probably about the same age.

I could've stood there and talked to her forever, but it was close to ten a.m. I knew if I wanted to get answers from Benjamin about who had called to meet with Victor, I had to do it early, before a lot of visitors came to the gallery.

CHAPTER SIXTEEN

After bidding farewell to Amelia, I crossed the street and approached Gallery 360. The early morning sun cast a warm glow on the storefront, enticing me to step inside. I tried the front door, but it was locked, reminding me that it wasn't yet opening time. Undeterred, I spotted a side door that was slightly ajar and slipped inside, hoping to catch an employee or at least Benjamin.

As I entered, the quietness of the gallery enveloped me. The main exhibition space was dimly lit, with artwork carefully arranged on pristine white walls. It was as if the room held its breath, waiting for the day to begin.

I couldn't help but notice a canvas on an easel in the middle of the room. I didn't remember this canvas from yesterday. A black cloth was draped elegantly along the top, spilling over the edges. When I got closer, I noticed the painting was a self-portrait done by Victor and that this was a type of memorial Gallery 360 had done in his honor.

A faint sound of music caught my attention, beckoning me farther into the gallery.

Following the melody, I ventured through an Employees Only door, curiosity guiding my steps. The back room unfolded before me, filled with an array of paints, brushes, and canvases. The air was tinged with a scent suggesting creativity, an intoxicating blend of linseed oil and pigments. This room was an artist's sanctuary, a place where imaginations ran wild on the canvas.

Lost in the scene, I failed to notice Benjamin, fully engrossed in his work, until I inadvertently startled him. With a gasp, he flung his paintbrush away, and time seemed to slow as it arced through the air, splattering paint in all directions. I instinctively raised my arms in defense, but it was too late. Paint splattered across my clothes, forming an abstract pattern that could rival any modern artwork.

In the midst of the chaos, Benjamin's eyes widened and his jaw dropped. "Oh my goodness! Violet! I am so sorry! I didn't see you there!"

I couldn't help but burst into laughter. The unexpected turn of events amused me to no end. "Don't worry, Benjamin. Consider it a collaboration between artist and journalist, a true masterpiece of the unexpected."

Benjamin's face transformed into a relieved smile. He must have realized the unintentional artistry in our mishap. "I couldn't have planned it better myself. It's a happy accident, a stroke of fate. How did you get in?"

"There was a side door slightly open." I tapped my temple. "Details are a journalist's kryptonite."

"I guess." He snickered and picked up a different paintbrush instead of going to get the one he'd flung at me like a weapon.

Surveying the paint-splattered room, I couldn't help but admire the chaos. Canvases stood against the walls, capturing Benjamin's artistic journey in bold strokes and vivid colors. Paintbrushes of all sizes were strewn about, standing like soldiers ready for battle. The scent of turpentine mixed with the aroma of fresh coffee, which Benjamin had evidently set aside in his creative fervor.

"It looks like you've been hard at work," I remarked, a smile playing on my lips. "These paintings are breathtaking."

Benjamin grinned, a touch of pride shining in his eyes. "Thank you,

Violet. It's a labor of love. Art has a way of bringing beauty into the world, even amidst chaos."

As we stood amidst the buzzing energy of the back room, paint-streaked clothes forgotten, I couldn't help but feel a kinship with Benjamin. Our unexpected encounter had brought us laughter and a sense of shared creativity.

"What are you doing here?" he asked, continuing to glide the brush over the canvas in a smooth motion.

I stood there in awe, waiting for him to give me a second without interrupting his creative process.

"Shouldn't you be covering the Fourth of July? It's the big last day. Miss Fourth of July is crowned later." He laughed, not caring a bit that it was our country's birthday.

"Oh!" I reached down in my bag and retrieved my phone. "I better tell Radley. I forgot, and Fern Banks will have my hide."

I walked away from his canvas, free from the paint-slinging process that he called art.

"I'm here to ask you about the conversation you had with the person who wanted to meet Victor at Brewing Beans." I hit the send button on the text to Radley, who quickly replied that he'd be more than happy to show up where Fern was going to be.

I sent back a thumbs-down.

Teasing.

Of course.

"Benjamin," I said, my voice shaking as I recounted Emily's narrative, "you have to tell me about the phone call. The one where you told Victor someone wanted to meet him."

His brush paused midstroke as his brow furrowed. "I'm afraid I don't know what you're talking about, Violet," he insisted again.

His nonchalance riled me up.

"Don't play games, Benjamin!" I snapped, my reporter's instincts in overdrive. "I know about the painting, about the forgery. The person who wanted to meet Victor after the Brewing Beans closed must be involved in his death and the missing painting."

The conversation spun me back to earlier interactions—Benjamin casually mentioning his travels, his passion for landscape painting, that he was one of Cassandra's students. The clues connected like a jigsaw puzzle forming an image I was reluctant to see.

As I paced around the gallery, my gaze flitted over numerous artworks until I noticed a hint of a familiar color, the edge of a canvas barely peeking out from underneath a dusty sheet. As I pulled the sheet away, my heart hammered against my ribs.

There it was—the missing landscape painting from Brewing Beans. The sight of it was a punch in my gut, solidifying my suspicions. My brain screamed at the revelation while a part of me denied the implication.

When I looked at Benjamin again, he was no longer painting. Instead, he was watching me, his countenance chillingly composed. Instead of holding a paintbrush, he was snapping a pair of latex gloves onto his hands with a calculated precision.

"I wish you hadn't snooped around, Violet." His voice was as cold as his eyes. "But your reporter's instincts have led you here."

My mouth went dry. "Benjamin... what are you..."

"Victor and Graham made a grave mistake," he said, his eyes devoid of any warmth they once held, "and it seems you're about to join them."

Before I could fully grasp the gravity of his words, he lunged at me. My thoughts spiraled into chaos as the terrifying reality settled in—Benjamin was the murderer.

CHAPTER SEVENTEEN

When I shielded myself from him, I fell to the gallery floor on my belly, clawing for my life as he tried to wrangle me into submission. His hands gripped around the back of my neck. I reached up over my head and grabbed a fist full of his hair, pulling it as hard as I could, causing him to screeched out in pain, voluntarily releasing his grip on me.

"I swear you're done for," he seethed through his gritted teeth and for a split second I saw his hands were up to his hair where the good chunk I'd pulled out now rested in my palm.

It was all in a few short seconds before I realized I was up on my feet and running to the door with the exit sign light up over the top of it.

"Call 9-1-1," I yelled out into my phone, the voice control recognized my voice as I pushed through the door.

I was never so happy to see the sunlight as I stood outside the gallery, gasping for breath and clutching my throat,

The sound of sirens grew louder in the distance. Relief washed over me as Chief Strickland's police car came into view and tore through the winding mountain roads. The urgency in the air was palpable.

When I heard the gallery door behind me pop open, I jerked around and Benjamin searched until our eyes met. I could see in his eyes he heard the sirens, then he closed the door, where no doubt he was going to go into hiding or find another way out.

I was not his victim.

Not today.

The vehicle screeched to a halt near the scene, and Chief Strickland jumped out, his eyes scanning the area. My hand instinctively rose to my throat, which still tingled from the close encounter with Benjamin's grip.

"Violet!" Darren's voice was filled with worry as he rushed to my side. His arms enveloped me in a reassuring embrace. "Are you all right? What happened?"

Amelia, who had followed the commotion from across the street, joined us, her eccentric presence adding a touch of color to the tense atmosphere. I took a deep breath.

"I found the missing painting, Darren," I said, my voice quivering with a mix of relief and excitement as I recounted the chain of events that led to this moment. "It was in the back room of Gallery 360, hidden under a sheet. Benjamin... He was the killer. I connected the dots, the conversations, and they all led me to him."

Chief Strickland emerged from the gallery, his face stern and resolved. He had Benjamin, who muttered and protested under his breath, in custody, though his defiance was fading in the face of imminent justice.

With a firm hand on Benjamin's arm, Chief Strickland led him toward the police cruiser. His voice authoritative, the chief said, "You're under arrest for the murders of Graham Winston and Victor Monroe. Anything you say can and will be used against you in a court of law."

While Benjamin was secured in the back of the cruiser, Darren's relieved expression softened, his gaze meeting mine.

"Thank goodness you're safe, Violet," he whispered, his voice filled with genuine concern. "Let's put this behind us and end the Fourth of July celebration on a high note. How about a magical night on the Ferris wheel?"

Before I could even answer him, the distant sound of the trolley dinged in the background. Just then, Goldie's trolley screeched to a halt, and Radley jumped out, his eyes bright with excitement.

"What on earth is going on? Your mama told me there was a call on the police scanner to Gallery 360, and I told her you were up here." Radley's eyes were wide.

"She caught the killer, dear," Amelia said, catching Radley's attention.

They made introductions, and I couldn't help but notice the twinkle of connection between Radley and Amelia. I shared a knowing glance with Darren, silently acknowledging the budding romance. I mentioned Amelia's delectable treats, and Radley's playful wink made her giggle.

"How about a ride?" Goldie had her hand on the lever of the trolley and leaned almost out of the door.

"Carnival, you two?" Darren pointed between Radley and Amelia.

"Let me get my purse." Amelia gleefully ran back across the street to the bakery. She hurried back, carrying a bag full of sweet treats for everyone.

Though I would have much rather gone home to bed, I knew it was probably best to enjoy the last night of the holiday with my new boyfriend and two new friends. Their company provided a comfort that I couldn't quite put my finger on.

Goldie pulled right up to the seaside where the big Merry Maker sign was located. I saw so many people I knew, including Mama and Daddy.

The bright lights and festive atmosphere invited us to create new memories and bid farewell to the Fourth of July with a bang. Together, we walked toward the laughter and joy that echoed through the night, leaving the darkness of the past behind us.

As the Ferris wheel carried Darren and me higher into the starlit sky, I couldn't help but feel a sense of hope and renewal. The mysteries of Holiday Junction had been unraveled, the truth exposed, and justice served. In the company of dear friends and the promise of a brighter future, we celebrated the triumph of good over evil, love over darkness, and the enduring spirit of Holiday Junction.

And as the Ferris wheel reached its pinnacle, our laughter mingled with the cheers and music of the carnival, a testament to the resilience and unity of our beloved town. In that fleeting moment suspended in time, I realized that even in the face of adversity, Holiday Junction would always find a way to shine, illuminating the path to a future filled with merriment, love, and endless possibilities.

A small smile tugged at the corners of my lips as I looked into Darren's eyes, grateful for his unwavering support. In that moment, the weight of the recent past began to lift, replaced by the promise of a joyous and carefree night.

.

Holiday Junction Shines Bright: Fourth of July Celebration Brings Merriment and Closure

Festivities and Unity Prevail as Murder Mysteries Are Solved

Violet Rhinehammer, *Junction Journal* Staff Writer

HOLIDAY JUNCTION, known for its charm and warm hospitality, concluded its Fourth of July celebration with a resounding success, showcasing the town's indomitable spirit. The streets were adorned with patriotic decorations, and the air was filled with laughter, music, and the mouthwatering aromas of delectable treats. As the sun set, a sense of togetherness enveloped the community, reminding us all that even in the face of adversity, Holiday Junction shines brighter than ever.

This year's Fourth of July celebration attested to our town's resilience as we came together to commemorate our nation's independence and celebrate the rich tapestry of our community. The festivities kicked off with a breathtaking parade in which vibrant floats, marching bands, and enthusiastic locals paraded through the streets. The energy was contagious, as families, friends, and visitors cheered, waving flags and reveling in the joyous atmosphere.

The beach carnival provided endless entertainment, with thrilling rides, captivating games, and food stands selling tantalizing fare that delighted the taste buds. The night sky was illuminated with a dazzling fireworks display, painting vivid streaks of color across the heavens, captivating young and old alike. Everyone present replied with oohs and aahs, showing the collective awe that echoed through their hearts.

However, the jubilation of the festivities was shadowed by recent events. Holiday Junction was rocked by the untimely deaths of two esteemed members of our art community, Graham Winston and Victor Monroe. The murders sent shock waves through our tight-knit town, leaving us questioning the safety and security we hold dear. But rest assured, the diligent efforts of our esteemed chief of police, Matthew Strickland, and his dedicated team have ensured that justice was swiftly served.

After an intensive investigation, the pieces of the puzzle fell into place, revealing a web of deceit and betrayal. Benjamin Clarke, a once-respected artist, was apprehended as the perpetrator of these heinous crimes. His arrest brings closure to the community, reminding us that Holiday Junction remains a safe and welcoming haven for residents and tourists alike.

Chief Strickland, in a press conference held earlier this week, assured the public that these tragic incidents were isolated and that our town continues to be a place of peace and tranquility. He extended his gratitude to the community for their support and cooperation throughout the investigation, emphasizing the importance of unity in times of adversity.

As we bid farewell to another successful Fourth of July celebration, Holiday Junction stands tall, a beacon of warmth, joy, and community spirit. We can once again revel in the knowledge that our beloved town remains a bastion of safety and serenity. With the spirit of the Fourth of July still burning brightly in our hearts, we look forward to the continued growth and prosperity of our cherished Holiday Junction.

In the words of Chief Strickland, "Let us remember that even in the face of darkness, the light of unity and resilience will guide us toward a brighter future."

CHAPTER EIGHTEEN

Holiday Junction: Where Merriment Reigns Supreme

By The Merry Maker

As the sun sets on another delightful chapter in the town of Holiday Junction, I can't help but feel a sense of joy and contentment. The Fourth of July festivities have come to a close, and our beloved village has once again lived up to its reputation as the epicenter of merriment.

The air was filled with laughter and cheer as residents and visitors alike gathered to celebrate the nation's independence. From the lively parade that wove its way through the streets, boasting colorful floats and spirited performers, to the grand fireworks extravaganza that lit up the night sky, every moment was infused with a sense of pure joy.

The spirit of Holiday Junction shone brightly throughout the week-long celebration, with our citizens embracing the merriment that defines our beloved village. From the enthusiastic participation in the annual pie-eating contest to the heartwarming performances at the community talent show, every event bespoke the joyous nature of our town.

But the celebrations don't end here, my dear friends. While the Fourth of July has bid us farewell, the merriment continues to thrive in every corner of Holiday Junction. Our quaint streets are once again bustling with activity, with locals and tourists embracing the warmth of our community.

And here's an exciting twist: I find myself intrigued by a new potential venture, a hidden gem nestled in the quiet embrace of the mountains. The art district, with its boundless creativity and unexplored potential, beckons to me. Could this uncharted territory hold the key to the next level of merriment for our beloved village? Only time will tell.

As I sign off, my dear readers, I leave you with a tantalizing thought. Keep your eyes peeled for the signs of the Merry Maker, for where there's merriment to be had, there just might be a clue to the next adventure. Who knows what surprises lie in store as we embark on this new journey together?

Until next time, my dear friends, embrace the spirit of Holiday Junction and let its merriment guide your way.

Yours in endless merriment,

The Merry Maker

THE END

If you enjoyed reading this book as much as I enjoyed writing it then be sure to return to the Amazon page and leave a review.

Go to Tonyakappes.com for a full reading order of my novels and while there join my newsletter. You can also find links to Facebook, Instagram and Goodreads.

Keep reading for a sneak peek of the next book in the series. Thanksgiving Treachery is now available to purchase on Amazon or read for FREE in Kindle Unlimited.

Chapter One of Book Seven
Thanksgiving Treachery

"To-furky," Millie Kay, my mama, harrumphed. "Who on earth ever heard of that?"

Her Southern twang garnered a snicker from Darren Strickland.

I glanced up from the list of activities I'd been curating, not as the *Junction Journal*'s editor in chief, my newest title, but as Holiday Junction's secret Merry Maker.

More correctly, I was the co–Merry Maker with Darren, but the title might'swell have been singular. He'd had his nose stuck in that book of his since he'd decided to go back to law school and start lawyering around here. That left me with the tasks involved in the centuries-old sacred job of deciding where in our little town each holiday's final hurrah would take place.

"You told me I could invite friends who lived in the art district," I reminded her, getting a smile from Darren, though his eyes were still laser-focused on the book in hand. "And I quote." I lifted a finger and said in my best Millie Kay voice, "'Now, Violet, I don't want anyone feeling left out for Friendsgiving. You go on and invite all them people up in the mountain and ask them what they like to eat so they can enjoy a nice friendly sit-down.'"

Mama had bought the old run-down building and had a grand idea of turning it into what she called a Leisure Center. Technically, the place was a senior citizen building with activities like bingo, line dancing, and now knitting classes—thanks to Amelia—as well as painting classes—again thanks to Amelia—among other pursuits mainly for people Mama's age.

Now Mama wasn't too old, but she was old for a mother when she had me, and that made her feel much older than her actual sixty-something years on this earth. She was Southern to her core, carrying the region's traditions with her in her personality, and that, my friends, truly made her an old soul.

Like with most things Mama did, she brought the color into any situation here in Holiday Junction.

"I thought they liked to eat turkey, stuffing, gravy, sweet potato casserole, buttermilk biscuits, cheesy grits, hash brown casserole... you know." She sighed as she picked up and shook the list of food Amelia Hartman had given me when I asked her for one. "Good food. Stick-to-your-ribs food. To-furky." She wadded up the paper and stood, tossing it in the trash can as she walked out of the dining hall and into the hallway. "I've got a meeting with Marianne Drew this afternoon. She's trying to move the Mistletoe Masquerade Ball and might rent the Leisure Center."

"Don't worry about the wadded-up guest list. I've got a copy," I said, smiling when she acted like she didn't hear me. She heard every single word I said and was no doubt off to find the fixings to make a Tofurky. But I was glad that she might get her first big rental out of Marianne Drew, a local woman I didn't know but who had already sent in information for me to do a big write-up in the *Junction Journal*.

I knew her by name but had never been face-to-face with her. In fact, I'd gotten another message last week from the desk of Mayor Paisley, asking if I could come to the last event of the Thanksgiving Festival. They were going to honor Marianne Drew with a Key to the Village due to her generosity.

"She's right, you know." Darren finally looked up, taking me out of my thoughts on how happy I was for Mama and what she'd done with this building.

No matter how much Darren stuck his head in those books, he surely didn't look the part of a lawyer in his wrinkled shirt with its long sleeves haphazardly rolled up or with his long hair that hung down in the back.

"That doesn't sound very appetizing at all," he said, his dark eyes almost hidden by his thick brows.

He smirked, knowing just how to push Mama's buttons.

"That's right," she agreed. Mama stuck out her tongue and then disappeared.

"You know what's not appetizing?" I glanced across the large community table. The afternoon sun filtered through the skylights, which were original to the old building.

The sunshine was very deceptive. If I were to walk outside of the Leisure Center, the weather would be much different.

Autumn had made what felt like an overnight rush into Holiday Junction.

Darren's comment about Tofurky still hung in the air as the amber light of late afternoon painted everything in warm hues. I couldn't help but gaze out of the Leisure Center's windows, momentarily lost in the beauty of Holiday Junction during this season.

"Holiday Junction is something else during the fall," I mused aloud, picturing the village in my mind.

The streets of our small village were lined with tall oak and maple trees, their leaves transforming into a tapestry of reds, oranges, and golds. It looked as though the mountains themselves caught fire in autumn, their slopes a riot of color, contrasting beautifully with the serene blue of the sea on the other side.

The countryside rolled out in stretches of harvested golden fields, dotted with pumpkins and chrysanthemums. Farmers would set up stands selling fresh apple cider, and children would run around, their laughter echoing as they jumped into heaps of raked leaves. The scent of burning wood would drift from chimneys, mingling with the ever-present aromas of baked goods and roasting nuts.

Local stores had already started their fall displays. Hand-knit scarves in seasonal colors hung in Emily's Treasure's shop window, and Brewing Beans had a sign promising the return of their famous pumpkin spice latte. Even the lampposts were wrapped in strands of orange and yellow fairy lights, creating a soft glow that would soon offset the season's earlier evenings.

"You know," I continued, turning back to Darren with a smile, "as much as Mama huffs and puffs about changes, there's something inherently comforting about the traditions here. The decorations, the food, the colors... It's all butter to the soul."

Darren chuckled, closing his law book for a moment. "Agreed. It's one of the reasons I've never left. Holiday Junction in the fall? There's nothing quite like it."

I nodded. As the *Junction Journal*'s editor in chief, I was fortunate to have a front-row seat to all the village's stories. But it was at times like this, during the embrace of autumn, that I felt a deeper connection.

Here, amidst the cozy traditions and the picturesque setting, was where stories truly came alive. And as the leaves fell, blanketing the village, I couldn't help but feel grateful to be right in the middle of it all.

"I'm really excited about Mama hosting Friendsgiving." I shrugged. "Maybe it'll be in the art district a little closer to the village."

I'd only really discovered the art district a few months ago. It was literally its own community, and from what I gathered and was still investigating, the two communities were always at odds with each other.

After I'd discovered the locals' attitudes, I took a vested interest in covering all the local government meetings as well as the chamber of commerce meetings, since the people there made most of the business decisions about shops and future mercantile endeavors.

Darren shifted from a seat at a corner table while a familiar smell drifted through the room.

The aroma of pumpkin spice from Brewing Beans reached us, and I took a deep breath, savoring the comforting scent.

"I'd only been in Holiday Junction a year, but that scent has quickly become synonymous with autumn," I remarked, thinking of how each year, the scent seemed to weave itself deeper into my memories. "We need to go down and see Hazelynn. She said everything was going fast," I said, talking about Hazelynn Hudson, the owner of and baker at Brewing Beans.

Darren looked over with a smile that was tinged with something else. He inhaled deeply, a look of nostalgia passing over his face.

"It reminds me of when I was a kid," he began, the distant gleam in his eyes showing he was years away. "Every fall, my mom would bring home a fresh-baked pumpkin pie and a steaming cup of pumpkin spice latte. The house would be filled with this aroma for days."

I nodded, appreciating the sentiment, since I could see his mama, Louise Strickland, doing those things for their family. She and Marge Strickland owned the *Junction Journal.* Marge was definitely not the mothering type Louise had been.

Something about this town and its traditions could quickly make anyone feel at home, but for those who grew up here, the connection ran even deeper.

Suddenly, Darren chuckled, drawing me from my musings. "Speaking of traditions, have I ever told you about the Leaf Dance?"

I shook my head, always eager to learn more about the intricacies of Holiday Junction.

"You should've seen it when we were kids," he said, his voice soft with remembrance. "Every year, as the trees began to shed their leaves, the entire town would gather in Holiday Park near the fountain. Kids, adults, everyone would dance and play, kicking up the fallen leaves, laughing and singing. The village would come alive with colors and stories from the elders."

I tried to picture the scene—the square alive with children laughing, elders sharing tales of yore, and the vibrancy of the autumn leaves swirling around the people. It sounded magical.

Darren's gaze became distant. "That was the essence of Holiday Junction," he continued. "It wasn't just about the decorations or the food. It was about the community coming together, sharing in the joys and traditions passed down through generations."

"We need to do that." I gasped, looking around to make sure no one was nearby to hear.

"What?" Darren snickered.

"As the you-know-whats," I whispered, my head cocked to the side and down to the ground, so no one would hear me as I discussed our Merry Maker duties with him.

"Oh," he said, smiling with a little glint in his eyes. "That's a great idea. The sign can be life-sized leaves in a dancing pattern." He used hand gestures to show how he envisioned Vern Mckenna was making the wood sign, which Darren and me set up in the wee hours of the morning without anyone seeing us.

"Help! Please, someone help!" Our conversation was shattered by a bloodcurdling scream, unmistakably Mama's.

Darren and I exchanged a glance of alarm before racing out of the dining area, our feet pounding the tile floor. The echoing scream seemed to come from the hall leading to the delivery entrance. We burst from the hallway and into the vicinity of the entrance's staircase, where we found a horrifying sight.

Mama stood there, her face pale, her trembling hands covering her mouth. At her feet lay Albert Harden, the kind man who had delivered milk to Holiday Junction residents for as long as I could remember. His body was crumpled awkwardly at the bottom of the steps leading to the loading dock. From where I stood, it looked like a tragic accident, like he had slipped while descending the steps to his delivery truck.

"Oh, Albert," Mama sobbed, her voice quivering. "I just came out to check on a delivery and... and there he was."

Darren moved quickly to Albert's side, checking for a pulse, while I took Mama into my arms and tried to soothe her racing heart.

"It's going to be okay, Mama," I whispered, though I wasn't sure of that. I took out my phone from my pocket and dialed 911.

"911. What's your emergency?" the operator asked.

Darren looked up, his expression grave. "He's gone, Violet."

A cold shiver ran down my spine.

Thanksgiving Treachery is now available to purchase or in Kindle Unlimited.

BOOKS BY TONYA
SOUTHERN HOSPITALITY WITH A SMIDGEN OF HOMICIDE

Camper & Criminals Cozy Mystery Series

All is good in the camper-hood until a dead body shows up in the woods.

BEACHES, BUNGALOWS, AND BURGLARIES
DESERTS, DRIVING, & DERELICTS
FORESTS, FISHING, & FORGERY
CHRISTMAS, CRIMINALS, AND CAMPERS
MOTORHOMES, MAPS, & MURDER
CANYONS, CARAVANS, & CADAVERS
HITCHES, HIDEOUTS, & HOMICIDES
ASSAILANTS, ASPHALT & ALIBIS
VALLEYS, VEHICLES & VICTIMS
SUNSETS, SABBATICAL AND SCANDAL
TENTS, TRAILS AND TURMOIL
KICKBACKS, KAYAKS, AND KIDNAPPING
GEAR, GRILLS & GUNS
EGGNOG, EXTORTION, AND EVERGREEN
ROPES, RIDDLES, & ROBBERIES
PADDLERS, PROMISES & POISON
INSECTS, IVY, & INVESTIGATIONS
OUTDOORS, OARS, & OATH
WILDLIFE, WARRANTS, & WEAPONS
BLOSSOMS, BBQ, & BLACKMAIL
LANTERNS, LAKES, & LARCENY
JACKETS, JACK-O-LANTERN, & JUSTICE
SANTA, SUNRISES, & SUSPICIONS
VISTAS, VICES, & VALENTINES
ADVENTURE, ABDUCTION, & ARREST
RANGERS, RVS, & REVENGE

CAMPFIRES, COURAGE & CONVICTS
TRAPPING, TURKEY & THANKSGIVING
GIFTS, GLAMPING & GLOCKS
ZONING, ZEALOTS, & ZIPLINES
HAMMOCKS, HANDGUNS, & HEARSAY
QUESTIONS, QUARRELS, & QUANDARY
WITNESS, WOODS, & WEDDING
ELVES, EVERGREENS, & EVIDENCE
MOONLIGHT, MARSHMALLOWS, & MANSLAUGHTER
BONFIRE, BACKPACKS, & BRAWLS

Killer Coffee Cozy Mystery Series

Welcome to the Bean Hive Coffee Shop where the gossip is just as hot as the coffee.

SCENE OF THE GRIND
MOCHA AND MURDER
FRESHLY GROUND MURDER
COLD BLOODED BREW
DECAFFEINATED SCANDAL
A KILLER LATTE
HOLIDAY ROAST MORTEM
DEAD TO THE LAST DROP
A CHARMING BLEND NOVELLA (CROSSOVER WITH MAGICAL CURES MYSTERY)
FROTHY FOUL PLAY
SPOONFUL OF MURDER
BARISTA BUMP-OFF
CAPPUCCINO CRIMINAL
MACCHIATO MURDER

Holiday Cozy Mystery Series

BOOKS BY TONYA

CELEBRATE GOOD CRIMES!

FOUR LEAF FELONY
MOTHER'S DAY MURDER
A HALLOWEEN HOMICIDE
NEW YEAR NUISANCE
CHOCOLATE BUNNY BETRAYAL
FOURTH OF JULY FORGERY
SANTA CLAUSE SURPRISE
APRIL FOOL'S ALIBI

Kenni Lowry Mystery Series

Mysteries so delicious it'll make your mouth water and leave you hankerin' for more.

FIXIN' TO DIE
SOUTHERN FRIED
AX TO GRIND
SIX FEET UNDER
DEAD AS A DOORNAIL
TANGLED UP IN TINSEL
DIGGIN' UP DIRT
BLOWIN' UP A MURDER
HEAVENS TO BRIBERY

Magical Cures Mystery Series

Welcome to Whispering Falls where magic and mystery collide.

A CHARMING CRIME
A CHARMING CURE
A CHARMING POTION (novella)
A CHARMING WISH

A CHARMING SPELL
A CHARMING MAGIC
A CHARMING SECRET
A CHARMING CHRISTMAS (novella)
A CHARMING FATALITY
A CHARMING DEATH (novella)
A CHARMING GHOST
A CHARMING HEX
A CHARMING VOODOO
A CHARMING CORPSE
A CHARMING MISFORTUNE
A CHARMING BLEND (CROSSOVER WITH A KILLER COFFEE COZY)
A CHARMING DECEPTION

Mail Carrier Cozy Mystery Series

Welcome to Sugar Creek Gap where more than the mail is being delivered.

STAMPED OUT
ADDRESS FOR MURDER
ALL SHE WROTE
RETURN TO SENDER
FIRST CLASS KILLER
POST MORTEM
DEADLY DELIVERY
RED LETTER SLAY

About Tonya

Tonya has written over 100 novels, all of which have graced numerous bestseller lists, including the USA Today. *Best known for stories charged with emotion and humor and filled with flawed characters, her novels have garnered reader praise and glowing critical reviews. She lives with her husband and a very spoiled rescue cat named Ro. Tonya grew up in the small southern Kentucky town of Nicholasville. Now that her four boys are grown men, Tonya writes full-time in her camper she calls her SHAMPER (she-camper).*

Learn more about her be sure to check out her website tonyakappes.com. Find her on Facebook, Twitter, BookBub, and Instagram

Sign up to receive her newsletter, where you'll get free books, exclusive bonus content, and news of her releases and sales.

If you liked this book, please take a few minutes to leave a review now! Authors (Tonya included) really appreciate this, and it helps draw more readers to books they might like. Thanks!

Cover artist: Mariah Sinclair: The Cover Vault

This book is a work of fiction. The characters, incidents, and dialogue are drawn from the author's imagination and are not to be construed as real. Any resemblance to actual events or persons, living or dead, is entirely coincidental. *Cover artist: Mariah Sinclair: The Cover Vault. Editor Red Adept.*